THE RYNOX MYSTERY

'THE DETECTIVE STORY CLUB is a clearing house for the best detective and mystery stories chosen for you by a select committee of experts. Only the most ingenious crime stories will be published under the THE DETECTIVE STORY CLUB imprint. A special distinguishing stamp appears on the wrapper and title page of every THE DETECTIVE STORY CLUB book—the Man with the Gun. Always look for the Man with the Gun when buying a Crime book.'

Wm. Collins Sons & Co. Ltd., 1929

Now the Man with the Gun is back in this series of COLLINS CRIME CLUB reprints, and with him the chance to experience the classic books that influenced the Golden Age of crime fiction.

THE DETECTIVE STORY CLUB

THE
RYNOX
MYSTERY

AN EXERCISE IN CRIME

BY

PHILIP MACDONALD

WITH AN INTRODUCTION BY
PHILIP MACDONALD

COLLINS
CRIME
CLUB

COLLINS CRIME CLUB
An imprint of HarperCollins*Publishers*
1 London Bridge Street
London SE1 9GF
www.harpercollins.co.uk

This edition 2017

1

First published in Great Britain by
W. Collins Sons & Co. Ltd 1930
Published by The Detective Story Club Ltd 1931

Copyright © Estate of Philip MacDonald 1930, 1963

A catalogue record for this book is available from the British Library

ISBN 978-0-00-824899-4

Typeset in Bulmer MT Std by
Palimpsest Book Production Ltd, Falkirk, Stirlingshire
Printed and bound in Great Britain
by CPI Group (UK) Ltd, Croydon CR0 4YY

INTRODUCTION

I WONDER how many professional storytellers can look back on their own early work with true objectivity. If there are any, I envy them. Because I know I can't. I always fall into the egocentric trap of disliking mine far too much; of feeling (as was once said of a friend of mine who was forever working on the great American novel and never finishing the first chapter) that 'it isn't good enough for me to have written.'

The only time I'm ever halfway satisfied with any work I've done is for a short while after I've finished it; a depressingly short and evanescent while. A week later any satisfaction with my labours is beginning to fade. In a month I am more than dubious. After a year, I'm convinced the whole thing smells to high heaven, and I can't imagine why anyone would ever trouble to read it.

But I realize that these are conditioned reflexes, and auto-conditioned at that, so I made up my mind to ignore them as I approached the task of going over the three books in this collection. But I still started on the job with trepidation; because (to be euphemistic) the tales were written some time ago* and I was terrified that, in spite of their original success, they might prove hopelessly out of date.

But somehow they didn't; and I was able to confine such editing as I did to matters of cutting, wording and style, of writing *qua* writing. Surprisingly, the stories themselves, as examples of three completely different types of what is now (unfortunately, I think) generically labelled 'Mystery Story', seemed to me to hold up pretty well: *The Rasp* as a pure, dyed-in-the-wool Whodunit; *Murder Gone Mad* as a tale of mass-murder, half Whodunit and half (to use a label of my own coining) Howcatchem; and *Rynox*, called a 'light-hearted thriller' at the time of its birth, as one of those razzle-dazzle,

---

* Not only a euphemism; an understatement verging on the classic.

now-you-see-it-now-you-don't affairs which many of us case-hardened toilers in the field of the *roman policier** like to throw off once in a while.

The Rasp was my third novel. It was also my first detective story,* and long before I'd finished it I was determined it should be my last. Conceived during a decade which was a Whodunit heyday, a time when it seemed that everyone in the storytelling business was trying his hand at the form, it was begun in a burst of youthful egotism, to show the world not only that I could do this too, but that I could do it better!

However, by the time I'd finished it I wasn't at all sure that I was showing anybody anything. All I knew was that this was hard, *hard* work; I had discovered that if the writer of *romans policiers* believes (as I think he has to) that his books should be novels as well as puzzles; that they must, always, be literate and credible as well as *scrupulously fair to the reader*, the writing of them is pure self-torture!

But—well, *The Rasp* made quite a splash when it came out, first in England and later in the US.† And I'm still torturing myself for a living, nowadays not only between book covers but also in the dramatic forms of film and television. Although I have, at various and several times, sought relief quite successfully in telling other sorts of story, I seem always to come masochistically back to the sweat and the frustration, the challenge and the agony, of working at what John Dickson Carr has called 'the greatest game of all'. And it might be worth noting that, when I do, I frequently use as my chief instrument a character (Anthony Gethryn) whom I never imagined, when I tucked him tidily away in matrimony at the end of *The Rasp*, would ever show his inquisitive and somewhat supercilious nose again . . .

---

* If labels must be used, I stubbornly prefer the old ones, unless I happen to invent them myself.

† Quite a while (!) after it was written, Ellery Queen did me the honour of including it in his definitive list of the 'Cornerstone' detective stories.

Now for *Murder Gone Mad*. This was my third or fourth detective novel, and is a very different cup of tea from the first. An attempt to break away from the then accepted, and terribly confining, limits of the pure Whodunit (blunt-instrumented corpse in copse or library—eight suspects—least likely murderer) it was suggested by the macabre but very real-life exploits of the greatest mass murderer of the century, the monster of Düsseldorf.

I'm not sure of my memory on this point, but I think I started the book with the idea that, as well as being a departure from the straight Whodunit form, it would also be easier to write. If I did think this, I was sadly mistaken. It was, in its own demonic way, every bit as tough to do. Because, after all, when the author (or policeman, if it comes to that) is faced with a clever and careful and *motiveless* killer, how *does* he set about uncovering him?

But the book got finished somehow and was very well received,* so I suppose I did all right by the theme, which is, after all, timeless. An interesting point, however, did occur to me while I was going over it; a point which might be worth some elaboration.

It concerns the present-day preoccupation with the psyche and all its widely bandied but only dimly understood *-iatrys* and *-opaths* and *-ologies*. If I were to be writing this book today, I believe I would feel bound to probe at length into the subconscious past of the murderer (in search, so to speak, of the *psora* and *trauma* of that dark district) so that I could eventually reveal that the whole trouble was caused by the fact that, at an early age, this unfortunate homicidal maniac (like the character in *Cold Comfort Farm*) had seen something nasty in the woodshed.

---

* In 1947, in a critical essay (the same as that from which I quoted him before) Mr John Dickson Carr actually included *Murder Gone Mad* as one of the all-time ten best detective stories.

But, in the days when I did write *Murder Gone Mad* I felt no such compulsion. It was enough, then, that the murderer was mentally unhinged; that the murderer was killing without sane motive; that the murderer was eventually caught . . .

That was the way we used to do it—and I'm not at all sure we weren't right . . .

This leaves *Rynox*. As I have already intimated, it is a much lighter book than the others; lighter in every way. Writing it was really a sort of busman's holiday; and, at the time, I almost had fun working on it, particularly since it satirized several persons and institutions in the London of that time—

I have just caught myself wondering whether the satire, unrecognizable here and now, was the only reason for the book doing as well as it did. And this means, I fear, that I'm back with my conditioned reflexes and had better stop, before I start saying, 'It isn't good enough for me to have written,' and thereby open the door temptingly wide for any critic who might feel like adding the words, 'or anyone else' . . .

PHILIP MACDONALD
in *Three for Midnight*, 1963

EPILOGUE

1

GEORGE surveyed the Crickford's man and the package with pompous disapproval.

'Bringing a thing like that to the front!' said George. 'Oughter know better. If you take your van down Tagger's Lane at the side there, you'll find our back entrance.'

George may have been impressive; was, indeed, to a great many people. But the vanman was not impressed. He evidently cared little for George's bottle-green cloth and gilt braid; less for George's fiercely-waxed moustache, or George's chest, medals or no medals.

'This unprintable lot,' said the vanman, ''as got this 'ere obscene label on it. My job ain't to stand 'ere chewin' the unsavoury rag with any o' you scoutmasters! My job's to deliver. Are you or are you not medically goin' to take unclean delivery?'

The normal purple of George's cheeks turned slowly to a rich black. George could not speak.

'If you don't,' said the vanman, 'gory well 'urry, off we go with the lot.' He stooped and looked at the label. 'And it's addressed to one of your big noises . . . F. MacDowell Salisbury, *Ess*quire. President: Naval, Military and Cosmo . . . Cosmos . . . whatever the 'ell it is, Assurance. That's you, ain't it?'

He held out a grimy thin-leaved book, together with a quarter-inch stub of unpointed pencil. A dark thumb pointed to the foot of the open page.

'You signs,' said the vanman, 'along dotted line 'ere, *if* you can write. Otherwise you'd better put your mark and I'll write somethink against it for yer. 'Urry up now!'

It will always be matter for conjecture as to what George would have done at this stage had not at this moment the car of F. MacDowell Salisbury drawn up immediately behind the Crickford's van. This left George only one course. Quickly he signed. Quickly he laid hold of the unwieldy package, which consisted of two large and heavy sacks tied together at the tops. With considerable exertion of his great strength he managed to drag them up the two remaining steps and in through the swing doors of glittering glass and mahogany. Just as, puffing, he had rested them against a corner of the panelled wall, the President came up the steps. George got to the door just in time; held it open; touched his cap; strove to keep his laboured breathing silent.

"Morning, George!' said the President.

George touched his cap again. He could not speak yet. The President was in good humour. Instead of striding straightway down the marble-floored corridor to the lift, he halted, his head on one side. He surveyed George.

'George,' he said, 'you look hot.'

'I am—*fuf*—sir!'

The President's eyes strayed to the unwieldy sacks. 'Weight-lifting, George?'

'Yessir. Just as you come, sir, I was telling the Crickford's man that he ought to 've took the lot round to the Lane entrance, but I saw it's for you, sir, so I brought it in this side.'

'For me?' The President's tone and his eyebrows went up.

'Yessir, according to the label.'

'Extraordinary thing!' The President walked over to the corner, bent down over the sacks and lifted the label. 'Extraordinary thing!' he said again. He put a podgy white hand to the joined sacks and tried their weight. 'Feels heavy,' he said.

'Heavy, sir,' said George, 'it is!'

Again the President stooped to the label. Yes, it bore his

name; also, in red ink and capital letters—staring capitals—the words:

'EXTREMELY PRIVATE AND
CONFIDENTIAL
PERSONAL FOR MR SALISBURY ONLY.'

'Well, I'll be damned!' said the President. 'Better get a couple of men and have it brought up to my office.'

2

The President, with fat white forefinger, pressed the third of the bell pushes upon his desk.

'Miss Winter,' he said, to the bell's genie, 'have they brought up those sacks?'

'The sacks have just come, Mr Salisbury.'

'Right! Just give the fellows a bob each out of the Petty Cash and then I'll come out. Most extraordinary-looking thing, isn't it, Miss Winter?'

'Yes, Mr Salisbury.'

Miss Winter, very severe, very neat, most efficient, went back to the outer office. The President, walking slowly after her, saw her distribution of largesse; saw the porters touching clean hats with dirty forefingers; saw the door close behind them; went out into Miss Winter's room.

Very untidily heaped in its very tidy centre were the sacks. Miss Winter was bending down, reading the label.

'Got a knife?' said the President.

Miss Winter had a knife. Miss Winter always had everything.

'Just see,' said the President, 'whether you can cut the string.'

Miss Winter could cut the string and did. The sacks fell apart. The President stirred one with his toe. The contents were hard, yet yielding.

'I can't make it out!' said the President.

'Shall I open a sack?' said Miss Winter. A very practical woman.

'Yes, yes. Let's have a look.'

Once more Miss Winter stooped; once more the penknife came into play as it ripped the stout thread which kept the mouth of the sack closed. Miss Winter inserted a hand . . .

'Good God!' said the President.

He took two short steps and stood at Miss Winter's shoulder. Upright again, she was holding between her hands a thick elastic-bound wad of one-pound Bank of England notes.

'Good God!' said the President again.

He bent himself over the mouth of the open sack and thrust in his own arm. His hand came away with yet another package . . .

He let the sack lie flat upon the floor, bent over it, caught it a little way down from its top and shook. Other packets fell from it upon the floor . . .

He looked into the sack . . .

There could be no doubt! The sack—it looked like a hundredweight-and-a-half corn sack—was filled, crammed, with bundles of one-pound Bank of England notes. They were not new, these notes. The bundles did not bear that solid, block-like appearance of unused paper money, but, although neat, were creased, and numbered—as Miss Winter at once was to find— in anything but series.

'Good *God!*' said the President. Himself, with Miss Winter's knife, he cut the threads which bound the mouth of the other sack. And this second sack was as its brother. If, indeed, there was any difference, it was that this second sack held still more bundles than the first. The President stood in the middle of the floor. Round his feet there lay, grotesque and untidy, little disordered heaps of money.

The President looked at Miss Winter. Miss Winter looked at the President.

'I suppose,' said the President, 'that I *am* at the office, Miss Winter? I'm not by any chance at home, in bed and fast asleep?'

Miss Winter did not smile. 'You certainly are at the office, Mr Salisbury.'

'And would you mind telling me, Miss Winter, what these things are that I'm treading on?'

'Certainly, Mr Salisbury. Bundles of one-pound notes, not very clean, I'm afraid.'

'I'm going back to my room to sit down,' said the President. 'If you wouldn't mind coming in again in a few minutes, Miss Winter, and telling me all over again what there is in those sacks, I should be very much obliged. Also you might empty the sacks and find out if there is anything else in them except . . . except . . . well, except bundles of one-pound notes!'

'Very well, Mr Salisbury. And would it not be as well, perhaps, if I also ring up Crickford's and see whether I can ascertain who is the sender of this, er . . . of this, er . . .' Even Miss Winter for once was at a loss for words.

'Do! Do!' said the President. 'And don't forget: come in and tell me all about it all over again!'

'Very well, Mr Salisbury.'

3

'If,' said F. MacDowell Salisbury to his friend Thurston Mitchell, who was Vice-President of the Naval, Military and Cosmopolitan Assurance Corporation, 'you can beat that, I shall be much surprised.'

Mr Mitchell could not beat it. He said so. 'If I hadn't,' said Mr Mitchell, 'seen the damn' stuff with my own eyes, I wouldn't believe you now, Salisbury . . . What did Crickford's say when Winter got on to them?'

'Crickford's,' said Mr Salisbury, 'agreed to make inquiries of their branches. They did. This package was delivered yesterday evening at their Balham Receiving Office. The customer, who did not give his name, paid the proper rate for delivery, asked when that delivery would be made, and . . .' Mr Salisbury shrugged his plump shoulders despairingly, '. . . just went.'

'What did he look like?'

'According to what Crickford's managing director told me on the phone, the clerk said that the sender was a "tall, foreign-looking gentleman." Little beard, broken English, rather exaggerated clothes—that sort of thing. Came in a car.'

'Car, did he?' said Mr Mitchell. 'Now did they . . .'

Mr Salisbury shook his head sadly. 'Mitchell, they did not. They couldn't tell me whether that car was blue or green, open or closed, English or American. They couldn't tell anything. After all, poor devils, why should they?'

Mr Thurston Mitchell paced the Presidential room with his hands in his pockets, his shoulders hunched, and a frown drawing his eyebrows together into a rigid bar across his high-bridged nose. He said:

'And there wasn't anything, Salisbury? Nothing in those sacks except money?'

'Nothing,' said the President. 'Nothing, Mitchell, of any description—except one grain of corn which I have here upon my desk. I thought I'd better keep it as a souvenir.'

'Well, I'm damned!' said the Vice-President.

'Quite,' said the President, 'probably . . . Yes, Miss Winter, what is it?'

Miss Winter came to the Presidential desk. There was about her a certain excitement, intensely restrained, but discernible nevertheless. She bore, rather in the manner of an inexperienced but imaginative recruit carrying a bomb, a small, oblong brown-paper parcel. She placed it upon the Presidential table. She said:

'This has just come, Mr Salisbury. By registered post. I thought I'd better let you have it at once because . . . well, because I fancy that the printing on it is the same as the printing on the sack label.'

The President stared. The Vice-President came to his shoulder and did the same thing.

'By Jove!' said the President. 'It is! Here, Mitchell, you open it. *You* haven't had a thrill today.'

The Vice-President, having borrowed Miss Winter's penknife, cut the parcel string, unwrapped three separate coverings of brown paper and found at last a stout, small, deal box. It had a sliding lid like a child's pencil-box. The Vice-President slid away the lid. He looked, and put the box down before the President. He said:

'Look here, Salisbury, if any more of this goes on, I shall go and see a doctor. Look at that!'

Mr Salisbury looked at that. What he saw was a sheet of white paper, and in the centre of the sheet of white paper a new halfpenny . . .

'Don't,' said the Vice-President, 'look like that, Salisbury. Damn it, you don't want any *more* money!'

The President removed the halfpenny and the sheet of paper. 'I've got it!' he said, 'whether I want it or not!'

Underneath the sheet of paper were, in three lines of little round stacks, forty-six new pennies. They were counted, with a composure really terrific, by Miss Winter. And underneath them was another piece of plain white paper. But this piece of plain white paper bore in its centre—neatly printed with a thick pen and in thick black ink:

'THIS IS THE BALANCE. THANK YOU VERY MUCH!

Total: £287,499 3s. 10½d....
(Two hundred and eighty-seven thousand, four hundred and ninety-nine pounds, three shillings and tenpence halfpenny.)
N.B.—Not for Personal Use. For the coffers of the Naval, Military and Cosmopolitan Assurance Corporation.'

The President looked at the Vice-President. Both looked at Miss Winter.

'Miss Winter,' said the President, 'would you be so very kind as to leave the room? I'm sure that in one moment Mr Mitchell will say something which it would be better for you not to hear.'

END OF EPILOGUE

REEL ONE

SEQUENCE THE FIRST

Thursday, 28th March, 193—   9 *a.m.* to 12 *noon*

ENTWHISTLE, the Fordfield postman, pushed his bicycle up the steep hill into Little Ockleton. The sack upon his back was heavy and grew heavier. The March sun, even at half-past eight this morning, seemed to carry the heat of July. Entwhistle stopped, puffed and mopped his head. He thought, as he thought every morning, that something ought to be done by the authorities about this hill. He pushed on again and at last was able to mount.

It was so rarely that he had a letter for Pond Cottage that he was nearly a hundred yards past it when he remembered that not only did he have a letter for Pond Cottage but that he had an unstamped letter for Pond Cottage. That meant collecting no less than threepence from Pond Cottage's occupier. The extra hundred yards which he had given himself was alleviated by the thought that at last—if indeed Mr Marsh were at home— he would see Mr Marsh and talk to Mr Marsh. He had heard so many stories about Mr Marsh and never had occasion to add one of his own to the many, that the prospect was almost pleasing. He dismounted, rested his bicycle against the little green paling and went through the gate and up the untidy, overgrown, flagged path.

Mr Marsh, it seemed, was at home. In any event, the leaded windows of the room upstairs stood wide.

Entwhistle knocked with his knuckles upon the door . . . No reply. He fumbled in his satchel until he found the offending, stampless letter . . . He knocked again. Again no answer came. Perhaps after all he was not going to see and talk with the exciting Mr Marsh. Still, one more knock couldn't do

11

any harm! He gave it and this time an answer did come—from above his head. An answer in a deep guttural voice which seemed to have a curious and foreign and throaty trouble with its r's.

'Put the dratted letters down!' said the voice. 'Leave 'em on the step. I'll fetch 'em.'

Entwhistle bent back, tilting his head until from under the peak of his hat he could see peering down at him from that open window the dark-spectacled, dark-complexioned and somewhat uncomfortable face of Mr Marsh. Mr Marsh's grey moustache and little pointed grey beard seemed, as Entwhistle had so often heard they did, to bristle with fury.

He coughed, clearing his throat. 'Carn' do that, sir,' he said. 'Letter 'ere without a stamp. I'll 'ave to trouble you for three-pence, sir.'

'You'll have to trouble me for . . . What the hell are you talking about? Put the damn letters down, I say, and get your ugly face out of here. Standing there! You look like a . . . Put the letters down and be off.'

Very savage, the voice was.

Entwhistle began to experience a doubt as to whether it would be quite as amusing to see and talk to Mr Marsh as he had supposed. But he stuck to his guns.

'Carn' do that, sir. Letter 'ere unstamped. 'Ave to trouble you for threepence, sir.'

'*Dios!*' said the voice at the window, or some sound like that. The window shut with a slam. Involuntarily Entwhistle took a backward step. He half-expected, so violent had been the sound, to have a pane of glass upon his hat. He stood back a little from the doorstep. He could hear quite distinctly steps coming down the creaking staircase and then the door was flung open. In the doorway stood a tall, bulky figure wrapped in a shabby brown dressing gown. Its feet were in shabbier slippers of red leather. The hair was black, streaked with grey. The moustache and little beard were almost white. The tinted glasses staring straight into Entwhistle's Nordic and bewildered eyes frightened Entwhistle. They gave to Entwhistle, though he could not have expressed this, a curious uneasy feeling that perhaps there were no eyes behind them.

'Where's this damn letter? Come on, man, come on! Don't keep me standing about here all day. It's cold!' The bulk of Mr Marsh shivered inside his dressing-gown. He thrust out an imperious hand.

Into this hand, Entwhistle put the letter. It was twitched from his fingers.

'I'll 'ave to trouble you for threepence, I'm afraid, sir.'

Mr Marsh made a noise in his throat; a savage animal noise; so fierce a noise that Entwhistle involuntarily backed two steps. But he stayed there. He stuck to his guns. He was, as he was overfond of saying, a man who knoo his dooty.

Mr Marsh was staring down at the envelope in his hands. A frown just showed above the tinted spectacles; white teeth below them glared out in a wild snarl. Mr Marsh was saying:

'Damn greaser!' and then a string of violent-sounding and most unpleasing words. He put his thumb, as Entwhistle watched, under the flap of the envelope and with a savage jerk freed its contents; a single sheet of typewritten paper. Mr Marsh read.

'F. X. Benedik,' growled Mr Marsh. And then another word. This time an English word which Entwhistle omitted when telling of the adventure to Mrs Entwhistle.

'I'll 'ave,' began Entwhistle bravely, 'to trouble you for . . .' There was a flurry within the door. It slammed. The violence of the slamming detached a large flake of rotting timber which fell at Entwhistle's feet.

Entwhistle pushed the postman's hat forward on to the bridge of his snub nose. The stumpy fingers of his right hand scratched his back hair. What, he wondered, was he to do now? It did not, it must be noted, occur to him to knock at the door again. Mr Marsh might be good gossip, but Mr Marsh was most obviously not the sort of man for a peace-loving postman to annoy. But there *was* the excess fee and when he got to Fordfield he would have to account for that. Well, threepence isn't much, but threepence is a half of Mild . . .

He was still debating within his slow mind when something—some hard, small, ringing thing—hit the peak of his cap with sharp violence. He started. The cap, dislodged by his jerk, fell off; rolled to the path. Bewildered, he looked down at it; stooped ponderously to pick it up. There beside it, glinting against a mossy flag, was a florin. Still squatting, Entwhistle looked up. The upstairs window was open again. From it there glared out Mr Marsh's face. 'It was,' said Entwhistle to Mrs Entwhistle that evening, 'like the face of a feen in 'uman shape. And,' said Entwhistle, 'he was laughin'. To 'ear that laugh would make any man's blood run cold, *and* I don't care 'oo 'e was. Laughin' he was; laughin' fit to burst hisself. What did I do? Well, I picks up the two-bob and me hat and I says as dignified like as I can: "You'll be requirin' your change, sir." Just like that I said it, just to show him I wasn't 'avin' no nonsense. What does 'e say? When he's finished laughin' a few minutes later, he says; "You can keep the something change and swallow it!" Funny sort of voice he's got—a *violent* sort of voice. That's what he says; "You can keep the something change and you can something well swallow it!" What did I say? Well, I says, still calm and collected like: "D'you know, sir, throwin' money like that, you might 'ave 'it me in the face," and then 'e says: "Damn bad luck I didn't!" just like that: "Damn bad luck I didn't! You something off now or I'll chuck something a bit heavier.".'

Thus the indignant Entwhistle to his wife. Thus, later that same evening, the histrionic Entwhistle in the bar of The Coach and Horses. Thus the important Entwhistle in the Fordfield police station three days later.

2

James Wilberforce Burgess Junior was whipping his top upon the cement path outside Ockleton station booking office.

James Wilberforce Burgess Senior, Ockleton's stationmaster, porter and level-crossing operator, watched for a moment with fatherly pride and then turned away to enter the hutch which was his booking office. He came out of the hutch a moment later a good deal faster than he had gone in. A sudden howl from James Wilberforce Junior had torn wailing way through the sunny morning.

James Wilberforce Junior was huddled against the wall with one hand at his ear and the other rubbing at his eyes. His top and his whip lay at his feet. Just within the doorless entrance was 'that there Mr Marsh.'

The Ockleton Burgesses have not, for many generations, been renowned for physical courage. Some fathers—however big, however sinister-seeming, the assaulter of their innocent child—would have hit first and spoken afterwards. Burgess did not hit at all. He said, instead, a great deal. That there Mr Marsh stood in the shadow, the odd, pointed black hat tilted forward upon his head. The dark glasses made pits in his face instead of eyes; his white teeth gleamed when he smiled his savage, humourless and twisted smile. He seemed to Burgess, no less than previously to Entwhistle, 'a feen in 'uman shape.' He cut presently across the whiningly indignant outburst of outraged fatherhood. He said:

'Cut it out! Cut it right out! I want a ticket for London.' His deep, somehow foreign voice boomed round the tiny brick box.

'Goin' about,' said James Wilberforce Burgess Senior, 'strikin' defenceless children! Don't you know it's dangerous to 'it a child on the yeerole?'

Mr Marsh took a step forward. Mr Burgess took three steps backwards. Mr Marsh pointed to the door of the ticket hutch. Mr Marsh said, and Mr Burgess swore afterwards that his teeth did not part when he said it:

'Into the kennel you go, little puppy. And give me a ticket for London.'

Here Mr Marsh, Burgess reported, put his hand into his pocket and pulled out half a crown which, with a half-turn of his body, he threw to the still snivelling James Wilberforce Junior.

'There,' he said, 'that'll buy him a new ear! Blasted kid!'

'All very well, sir,' said Burgess, now speaking through the pigeon-hole, 'walking about, striking defenceless children . . .'

Into the pigeon-hole Mr Marsh thrust his dark face.

'Give me,' said Mr Burgess afterwards, 'a fair turn, sort of as if the devil was looking at you through a 'ole.'

Mr Marsh received his ticket. Mr Marsh was presently borne away by the 9.10 Slow Up from Ockleton. He had bought a day-return ticket.

Upon the Ockleton platform that night, there waited for Mr Marsh's return not only James Wilberforce Burgess Senior but James Wilberforce Burgess Senior's sister's husband, one Arthur Widgery. This was a big and beery person whose only joy in life, after beer, was performing the series of actions which he invariably described as 'drawin' off of 'im and pastin' 'im one alongside the jaw!'

But Mr Marsh did *not* take advantage of the return half of his ticket.

3

Mr Basil Musgrove, who had charge of the booking office of the Royal Theatre, was this morning presenting an even more than usually bored exterior to the world. Last night Mr Musgrove had been out with a set of persons to whom he referred as the boys. Consequently Mr Musgrove, underneath his patent leather hair, had a head which was red hot and bumping.

Mr Musgrove said into the telephone: 'No, meddam. We do not book any seats at all under three shillings!'

Mr Musgrove said, to a purply-powdered face peering in through his pigeon-hole: 'No, meddam, we have no stalls whatsoever for this evening's performance. I am sorry.'

Mr Musgrove, when the face had vanished, put his head upon his hand and wished that the boys would not, quite so consistently, be boys. Mr Musgrove's heavy lids dropped over his eyes. Mr Musgrove slept.

Mr Musgrove was awakened most rudely. Something cold and sharp and painful kept rapping against the end of his nose. Mr Musgrove put up feeble hands to brush this annoyance away, but, instead of being brushed away, its rappings grew more frequent and really so discomfortable that Mr Musgrove's eyes were forced to open. With the opening of his eyes, the world came back with a rush. Mr Musgrove had been sleeping at his job! He saw now what it was that had awakened him. It was the ferrule of an ebony walking-stick. He looked down this stick. The ferrule was now hovering barely half an inch from the end of his nose. Peering round the stick, he saw a strange unusual sight; a pair of dark goggling, blank eyes set in a face which, he told some of those boys the next night, was just like Old Nick looking at you . . .

Mr Musgrove drew back with a start. His chair tilted underneath him and he narrowly escaped a fall.

The walking-stick was withdrawn. The window now was filled with this devil's head under the strange, pointed black hat; there were dark glasses; a little grey block of beard; a white, twisted, inimical smile.

'Er . . .' said Mr Musgrove, 'er . . . er . . . I beg . . . er . . .'

The stranger said a word. And then: 'Any stalls tomorrow night?'

'No. No,' said Mr Musgrove, 'no, no, no!'

'I heard,' said the stranger, 'what you said the first time.'

Mr Musgrove strove to collect his scattered wits. 'No, sir.

No. We are entirely full for both the matinee and the evening performance today.'

The face seemed to come nearer. It was almost through the pigeon-hole. Mr Musgrove recoiled; once more felt his chair rock beneath him.

'I didn't,' said the harsh voice, which seemed to find trouble with English r's, though none with English idiom, 'I didn't ask for today's performance. I asked about *tomorrow*!'

'Oh! Er . . . I'm sorry!' Mr Musgrove babbled. 'I'm sorry. I'm afraid I didn't catch what—'

'Cut it out! Have you or have you not three stalls for tomorrow night's performance?'

'Tomorrow, sir, tomorrow?' said Mr Musgrove. 'Three stalls, sir, three stalls. Would you like them in the middle, sir, at the back, or in the front at the side . . . I have a nice trio in H—'

'I don't care,' said the voice, 'in the least where the hell the damn seats are! All I want is three stalls. Give 'em to me and tell me how much they are so that I can get away from your face. It's not a pleasant face, I should say, at the best of times. This morning it's an indecency.'

Mr Musgrove flushed to the top of his maculate forehead. The tips of his ears became a dark purple colour. As he said to the boys that evening: 'D'you know, you chaps, if it had been any other sort of man, well, I'd have been out of that office and set about him in half a second. You know me! But as it was, well, believe me or believe me not, I just couldn't move. I was rooted! All I could do was to give him his three seats and take his money. You see some odd customers in my job, but I've never seen such an odd one as that before *and* I don't want to see another one like it. Horrible old bloke! Sort of nasty, sinister way to him, and what with that beard and those dark glasses and that limp—he sort of seemed to drag his left leg after him and yet go pretty fast—he was a horrible sort of chap! I'm going to look out for him tomorrow night and see what sort of company he's got . . . Thanks, Ted; mine's a port and lemon. Cheerioski!'

COMMENT THE FIRST

NOT a pleasant person, Mr Marsh. Little Ockleton—where he has had a weekending cottage for the past six months—cannot abide him. Nor can any one, it seems, with whom he comes into contact. And how he dislikes having to pay excess postage— or was that outburst more by reason of his feelings towards the sender of that particular letter?

SEQUENCE THE SECOND

Thursday, March 28th, 193—   12.30 *p.m. to* 3.30 *p.m.*

THE offices of RYNOX (Unlimited) are in New Bond Street. A piece of unnecessary information this, since all the world knows it, but it serves to get this Sequence started.

Up the white marble steps of Rynox House—RYNOX themselves use only one floor in the tall, narrow, rather beautiful building—there walked, at 12.30 in the early afternoon of this Thursday, Francis Xavier Benedik—'F. X.' to his many friends and few but virulent enemies.

The door-keeper, a thin, embittered person with the name of Butterflute, smiled. The effort seemed—as F. X. had once indeed remarked—to sprain the poor man's face. But smile he did. Everybody smiled at F. X.—except those few but very bitter enemies. F. X. paused upon the top step.

''Morning, Sam,' he said.

'Good-morning, sir,' said Butterflute.

'How's the sciatica?'

'Something chronic, sir.'

'That's a bad job. How's the family?'

'Not too well, sir,' said Butterflute. 'Wife's confined again; *I* dunno 'ow she does it! Me boy got three weeks yesterday, for D. and D. in charge of a motor car, and me daughter—well, sir—'

F. X. was grave and sympathetic, also determined. 'Damned hard luck, Butterflute. Damned hard! Anything you want, just let me know, will you?'

Butterflute touched his cap. 'Yes, sir. I will that, sir. Thank you, sir.'

F. X. went on and through the main doors and so along the

corridor to the lift; a tall, burly but trim, free-striding figure
which might have been from the back that of an athletic man
of thirty. It was only when you saw his face that you realised
that F. X. was a hard-living, hard-working, hard case of fifty-
five. You realised that, and you were quite wrong. Wrong about
the age, anyhow, for this day was the sixty-seventh birthday of
Francis Xavier Benedik. But whatever your guess, whoever
you were—unless indeed you were one of those few but very
violent enemies—you loved F.X. on sight. He was so very much
the man that all the other men who looked at him would have
liked to have been. He had obviously so much behind him of
all those things of which, to be a man, a man must have had
experience.

"Morning, sir!' said Fred. Fred was the liftboy. In direct
contrast to Butterflute Fred did not smile. You see, Fred otherwise always smiled, but Fred felt, as every one, that one must
do something different for F.X. So instead of smiling, Fred
looked grave and important.

"Morning, Frederick! Lovely day!'

'It is that, Mr Benedik, sir. Beautiful day.'

The lift purred softly and swiftly upwards. Frantic would-be
passengers on the first, second and third floors were passed
with a cool contempt. Had not Fred got RYNOX in his lift!

The lift stopped. For other passengers Fred was wont to jerk
the lift, being the possessor of rather a misguided sense of
humour, but for F. X. Fred stopped the lift as a lift should be
stopped; so smoothly, so gently, so rightly that for an appreci-
able instant the passenger was not aware of the stopping.

At the gates F. X. paused. He said over his shoulder:

'You look out for that girl, Frederick.'

From between Fred's stiffly upstanding cherry-coloured
collar and Fred's black-peaked cherry-coloured cap, Fred's face
shone like a four o'clock winter sun.

'Beg pardon, sir?' said Fred. 'Which girl was you meanin',
sir?'

'You can't tell me, Fred! That little dark one; works on the first floor. Between you and me, you might tell her that their Enquiries door wants a coat of paint, will you? . . . She's all right, Fred, but you want to look out for that sort with black eyes and gold hair.'

The winter sun took on an even deeper shade.

'Oh, Fred!' said F.X.

The lift shot downwards at the maximum of its speed.

Past the big main doors upon this top floor—the big doors with their cunningly blazoned sign:

RYNOX

S. H. RICKFORTH   ANTHONY X. BENEDIK

F. X. BENEDIK

went F. X., with his long, free stride which seemed somehow out of place in a city. Past these and past the next small door bearing the sign:

RYNOX

ENQUIRIES HERE

and so to the modest mahogany door—the door which most people passing along this corridor thought was that of a lavatory. The handle of this door turned in F. X.'s fingers. He went in, shutting the door behind him.

''Morning, Miss Pagan. 'Morning, Harris.' Thus F. X., hanging up his light grey, somehow dashing-looking hat.

'Good-morning, Mr Benedik,' said Miss Pagan, her sad, blond beauty illumined by one of her rare smiles.

''Morning, sir,' said Harris.

'Mr Rickforth in, Miss Pagan?'

'Yes, Mr Benedik. I think he's in your room. He said he wanted to see you particularly before you started work.'

'Mr Anthony here?'

'Not yet, Mr Benedik. Mr Anthony wired from Liverpool that he was coming in on the twelve-fifty; would you wait lunch for him?'

F. X. crossed the room, stood with his fingers upon the baize door which separated this outer office of his from the corridor leading to the partners' rooms.

'Anything else, Miss Pagan?' he said. 'I don't want you to come in with the letters just yet. Wait until I've seen Mr Rickforth.'

'Very well, Mr Benedik.' Another of Miss Pagan's rare and sadly beautiful smiles. 'No, nothing else except Mr Marsh.'

A frown marred the pleasantness of the senior partner's tanned face. 'Marsh,' he said. His voice grated on the ear. 'Has he been bothering you?'

Miss Pagan shrugged elegant shoulders. 'Well, not bothering, Mr Benedik, but he's rung up twice this morning; the second time only five minutes before you got here. He seems to want you very urgently.'

'Ever know him,' growled F. X., 'when he didn't want to see me very urgently?'

Miss Pagan shook her blond head. 'I've never seen Mr Marsh, Mr Benedik. I must say, though, on the telephone he always does sound cross.'

'Crosser than his letters?' said F. X.

'That,' said Miss Pagan, 'would be impossible . . . Anyhow, he said would you please telephone him as soon as you got here.'

F. X. raised his eyebrows. 'Number?' he said.

'I asked him for the number, Mr Benedik, and he wouldn't give it.' Miss Pagan's eyebrows suggested that Mr Benedik should know by this time what Mr Marsh was like. 'All he'd say was "the Kensington number".'

F. X. laughed, a snorting contemptuous laugh. 'That's like the fool!' he said. 'All right, I'll get on to him. I'll see Mr Rickforth now. I'll ring when I want you, Miss Pagan.'

2

'But good gracious me!' said Rickforth. 'My dear Benedik, I daresay that I have not your push, your ability to handle big things courageously, but I do know, and I think that you know too, that I'm a man with a certain amount of business knowledge, and what I say, Benedik—'

F. X., whose gravity throughout this interview had amounted to more than sadness, suddenly grinned. The whole man, with that flash of white teeth, shed twenty hard-fought years. He said:

'Sam, my boy, when you clasp your hands over that pot-belly of yours and start calling me Benedik, I can't help it, but I want to kick your bottom. You know, Sam, the trouble with you is that you've got the ability of a Hatry, the tastes of a sexless Nero, and the conscience of an Anabaptist minister. You're a mess, Sam, an awful mess, but you're not a bad fellow as long as you don't hold your belly and call me Benedik, and'— momentarily the smile faded—'and as long as you don't try to teach F. X. Benedik his job. Good Lord, man, don't you think that I know what state the business is in? You seem to forget, as a matter of fact, that I *made* the damn business. I know how deep we are in it, but I know, too, how high we're going to soar out of it after this waiting business is over, so for God's sake stop moaning. If you want to get out, get out! Go for a holiday or something. Go and hold your belly in a cinema. Don't come here and try to make that fat face of yours all long. I can't stand it and I won't!'

Samuel Harvey Rickforth laughed; but it was a laugh that had in it an undercurrent of fear.

'My dear F. X.,' he said, 'I'm not being what I suppose you'd call "a wet sock." I'm merely trying to show you the sensible point of view. RYNOX gave up practically all their other interests for the Paramata Synthetic Rubber Company. You did it. You backed your own judgment and we, very naturally, followed you. But even at the time—at the beginning, I mean—I freely confess I got nervous. I thought to myself, can he pull it off? . . . What's the matter? . . .'

F. X. had sunk into an armchair of deep and yielding leather. His long legs were thrust stiffly out before him. A large white silk handkerchief covered his face. His hands were folded over his chest in the manner of a sleeping Crusader. From under the handkerchief his voice came hollow:

'Nothing's the matter. Go on, Samuel, go on!'

Again Rickforth laughed. 'It's all very well,' he said, 'but I will finish. It's my opinion, F. X., and I'm not joking, that you've done what you'd call "bitten off more than you can chew." Look at us, overdrawn here, overdrawn there; creditors beginning to get uneasy, and what are we waiting for? Orders that may come but equally may not, and . . . and . . .' His fat, well-to-do voice grew suddenly sharp. 'And, F. X., RYNOX is unlimited! You would have it, and it is, and whereas I might not say all this if we were a limited company, as a partner in an unlimited company I must say all this.'

The handkerchief flew a foot into the air as F. X. let out his pent breath. Suddenly he hoisted his bulky length from the chair, took two steps, and clapped a lean brown hand—which to Samuel Harvey Rickforth felt like the end of a steel crane— upon Samuel Harvey Rickforth's shoulder.

'My dear Sam!' said F. X., 'if you don't know me by this time well enough to know that I wouldn't let a blue-nose go into your house and sell your glass while you're drinking out of it, you're an old fathead! Now, for God's sake, go out, buy yourself a couple of bottles of Pol Roget '19 and charge 'em down to the travellers' expenses. And when you come back, for God's sake come back cheerful. I've got enough troubles without seeing those podgy hands of yours clasping that obscenity you call a stomach. What you wear those buff waistcoats for, I can't make out! They only accentuate it. What you want, Sam, is a bit more of your daughter's spirit. If I were to tell Peter what you've been saying this morning—'

'I say, F. X., you wouldn't do that, would you?' Mr Rickforth was alarmed.

F. X. put back his head and laughed. 'By God, Sam! I believe I've got you!' he said. 'I haven't tried it before, but I'll try it now. If I have any more of this S.O.S. stuff, I'll tell Tony and then you'll get it hot all round. Now, buzz off, you old blight!'

Rickforth went, but the door was only just closed behind him when it opened again. It admitted his round pink-and-white face, somehow frightened-looking under the ivory white sheen of his baldness.

'I say, F. X.' said the face, 'you won't really tell Peter, will you? I mean, damn it, business is business . . .'

The 193— edition of the Directory of Directors smote the door with all its half-hundredweight of matter one-tenth of a second after Samuel Harvey Rickforth had closed it.

F. X. reached out for the telephone; picked it up; lay back in the chair with the receiver at his ear and the body of the instrument cuddled closely against his chest. He always spoke. like many men who have lived at least half their lives, in very different places from city offices, very loudly over the telephone. 'Kensington,' he shouted, 'four-double-nine-nine-oh . . . Is that Kensington four-double-nine-nine-oh? . . .' His voice was thunderous. 'Can I speak to Mr Marsh? . . . Eh? . . . What's that? . . . Mr Marsh, I said. M for Marjorie, A for Ambrose Applejohn, R for rotten, S for sausage, H for How-d'ye-do . . . Marsh . . . Oh, right. I'll hold on.'

He reached out a long arm, the receiver still at its end, and pressed that one of the buttons on his desk which would bring Miss Pagan. When Miss Pagan came he was talking again. He was saying:

'Well, certainly, we've got to get this matter settled. I can't make you see reason by writing, so I suppose we'd better meet. Now, I'm very busy. I suggest we should meet some evening, as soon as you like. Not tonight. I've got a dinner party. Tomorrow night, say. Just a moment, I'll ask my secretary . . .

All right, keep your shirt in! Keep your shirt in! Keep letting it hang out like that and you'll be arrested for exhibitionism.'

He looked up from the telephone, clasping the mouthpiece firmly to his waistcoat.

'Miss Pagan,' he said, 'got my book?'

'Yes, Mr Benedik.' Miss Pagan's tone was faintly injured. Of course she had his book.

'Am I doing anything tomorrow night?'

'There's nothing in *this* book, Mr Benedik.'

'Well, I don't know of anything,' said Benedik; then into the telephone: 'Marsh, still there? . . . Look here, Marsh, I'm free tomorrow night. Come along to my house and see me, will you? And I want to assure you that we're going to settle. You worry the life out of me and you worry the life out of my people and your voice is beastly over the telephone anyhow! Understand what I'm talking about? I'm going to *settle*! Are you free tomorrow night? . . . Right, ten o'clock suit you? . . . Right. Well, come to my place ten o'clock . . . What's that? . . . You great sap, you know damn well where I live. Oh, well, perhaps you're right, perhaps I never told you; thought you might come round worrying the servants or something. 4 William Pitt Street, West one . . . No, Mayfair . . . Yes, come through the market if you're coming from the Piccadilly side. Four. That's right . . . Right, ten o'clock tomorrow night. Good-bye!'

He replaced the receiver with a savage click; set the telephone down upon his desk with a bang. 'And,' he said, looking at it, 'God blast you!' He looked up at Miss Pagan. 'Shove that down, will you? Ten p.m., house—for tomorrow this is, you understand—ten p.m., house, Marsh. And put it in big red capital letters. And I'd like to tell you this, Miss Pagan, that if ever that'—he drew a deep breath—'if ever that person—I can't say more in front of a gently nurtured English girl—if ever he puts his wart-hog's nose in this office after tomorrow night, you have my instructions to crown him with the heaviest thing you can lay your hands on. And if he rings up, ring off . . . Mr Anthony back yet?'

'Not yet, Mr Benedik. Shall I ask him to come and see you as soon as he gets in?'

'Please,' said F. X. 'And now you might bring me that last lot of composers' reports from Lisbon, and tell Mr Woolrich to come and see me.'

The Lisbon reports had been brought and read and digested before Woolrich came. Twice F. X., now alone, had looked at his watch before there came a soft tapping upon the door and round its edge Woolrich's sleek fair head.

F. X. looked up. He said:

'Enter Secretary and Treasurer with shamefaced look. And you'd better hurry, too.'

Woolrich came in.

'I'm awfully sorry, sir,' he said. 'Afraid I missed my train this morning. I'd been down to . . . down to . . . to the country.'

F. X. looked at him. F. X., after one frosty instant, smiled. 'You're always,' he said, 'going down to the country. You know, Woolrich, you ought to be careful of that country. I'm not sure it's doing you much good . . . in fact, if you weren't such a damned good man I should have a great deal more to say about the country . . . Sit down!'

Woolrich moved over to the big chair at the far side of the desk. He was a tall and broad-shouldered and exquisitely-dressed person of an age difficult to determine. He might have been anything between twenty-five and forty. Actually he was thirty-six. His tan was as deep almost as F. X.'s own, and his ash-blond hair was bleached by the sun and open air . . . but under the startlingly blue eyes were dark and lately almost permanent half-moons.

'Look here, Woolrich!' F. X. leaned forward. 'I've just been looking over this last lot of reports from Lisbon. I expect you've read 'em.'

Woolrich nodded. 'I think,' he said, 'I could say them over by heart.'

'You mean,' said F. X., 'you know you could . . . Look here, there's only one thing that worries me, and that's Montana. You know and I know that Montana's not square—unless it pays him to be—and is it paying him?'

Woolrich nodded. He said, with emphasis:

'It is. If he went over to real rubber he'd never get the money. There aren't any flies on Montana. You know that, sir, and he must realise that if he started any double-crossing he might do well for a bit but in the long run he'd get ditched. I've thought it all out.'

'That,' said F. X., 'is my opinion too . . . All right, we'll leave that at that. Now . . .'

They plunged into many and intricate details of business. They did, in ten minutes, so used were they to each other, as much work as most other couples in London, standing in the same relation, would have spent two hours and more upon.

F. X. rose and stretched himself. His big body seemed suddenly to tower. He said:

'Well, that's that! Anything else, Woolrich?'

Woolrich pondered a moment. His blue eyes narrowed as he thought and one corner of his well-cut, clean-shaven mouth twitched to a little constricted grin of concentration. At one corner of this mouth there showed a gleam of teeth as white as F. X.'s own. He pulled out a small notebook; flipped over its pages.

'Nothing today, sir.'

'You don't want,' said F. X., looking at him keenly, 'to go down to the country this afternoon?'

A dark flush darkened Woolrich's tan. He shook the blond head. 'No, sir.' He stood up. 'If there's nothing else I'll go and have a bite of lunch. Busy afternoon after what we've done.'

F. X. nodded. 'No, there's nothing else.'

Woolrich walked to the door. With his fingers on its handle he turned. He said:

'By the way, sir, I hear that fellow Marsh has been ringing up—'

'Oh, him!' said F. X. 'That was before you came . . . All right, don't blush. I meant to tell you, Woolrich, I've made an appointment with Marsh for tomorrow night. I'm going to meet him after all. And I'm going to settle with him.'

Woolrich came away from the door, back into the centre of the room.

'Good Lord, sir!' he said. 'You don't mean to say you're going to—'

F. X. shook his head. 'No, no, no! Woolrich, I'm not wringing wet—you know that. No, I'm going to tell Mr Marsh that if he likes to take a little douceur he can buzz off; if he doesn't like to take it, he can buzz off just the same. I'm fed up with him . . . And if after tomorrow he ever rings up or shoves his face in here again, you can have him buzzed off with my love. Anyhow, we don't want things like that blocking up the place.'

Woolrich paused on his journey to the door. He said:

'I've never seen him, sir, and I don't want to. But from what you said I should imagine you're right.'

'I am!' said F. X., with feeling. 'Anthony here yet?'

'I'll send him along, sir,' said Woolrich, and was gone.

3

Francis Xavier Benedik and Anthony Xavier Benedik stood expectant just within the main doors of the Alsace Restaurant. They were waiting for Peter. Peter Rickforth was Samuel Harvey Rickforth's daughter and did not look it. She was also—or perhaps primarily—the future wife of Anthony Xavier Benedik. She was very, very easy to look at. Her engagement to Tony Benedik had broken, at least temporarily, more hearts than any feminine decision in London for the past six months.

Peter was always late. Tony looked at F. X. 'I think,' said Tony, 'another little drink.'

'That'll be three,' said his father.

'Right-ho, if you say so!'

They drank standing, their eyes fixed upon the revolving doors through which Peter would presently come. Standing there, utterly unconscious of their surroundings, glasses in hands, they were a couple which brought the gaze of many eyes to bear upon them. Exactly of a height, exactly of a breadth, with the same rather prominent-jawed, imperious nosed, hard-bitten good looks, the same deep, wide shoulders and narrow horseman's hips, they were a walking, talking proof that heredity is not an old wife's tale. What lineage, God knows, for F. X. himself could scarcely tell you from whence he came, but wherever this was, it and his own life had stamped their stamp upon the man, and this stamp was upon the son. They did not, these two, behave like father and son. They were more like elder and younger brother—much more. In only one particular was their aspect different. In the dress of F. X. was a careless, easy mixture of opulent cloth and 'I-like-a-loose-fit-blast-it-what-do-clothes-matter?' carelessness. In the dress of Tony was a superb and apparently unconscious elegance.

The revolving doors revolved. The little negro page-boy smiled until his face looked like an ice pudding over which chocolate has unevenly flowed.

'Mawnin', miss!' said the page-boy.

''Morning, Sambo!' said Peter Rickforth. She looked about her. She did not have far to look. Father and son were straight before her. She came towards them with her hands outstretched.

'My dears,' she said, 'do not—do not say all those things which are trembling on your tongue and shooting darts of fire from your too amazingly similar pairs of eyes! I'm sorry! I'm sorry! And I'm sorry! How's that?'

'Very well,' said F. X. 'In fact, Peter, I think you are too well-mannered. After all, you know, any couple of men ought to be only too damn glad for you to lunch with them at all, let alone worry if you're a few minutes late.'

'Few minutes!' said Tony. 'Few minutes! If you do this, my

girl, after we're married, you'll only do it once. At least, only once a month.'

Peter's golden eyes stared at him. 'Only a month? Why only once a month? Why not once a week?'

'The effects,' said Tony, 'of the beatings will last three weeks, five days and seven hours exactly. We've got a table. Shall we go in, F. X.?'

'If,' said his father, 'the lady wills.'

The lady did will, and presently they sat, a trio to draw all eyes, over a meal which was probably for that one day at least the best of its kind in all London.

It was over coffee that F. X. said:

'Peter, I want to talk to you about your family.'

Peter laughed. 'Family, sir?' she said. 'It's the first I know about it!'

'I mean,' said F. X., 'the other way round, backwards. Your father.'

'Oh, *Daddy*!' said Peter. 'What's he been doing? You don't mean to tell me that squinting one in the Palazzo chorus has been getting Daddy into trouble, do you? She does squint, you know. She's got the most *awful* cast in one eye!'

'My good girl,' said Tony, 'you want a twisted snaffle in that mouth of yours.'

'Your father, Peter,' said F. X., 'said nothing to me about squinting Palazzo's. Nothing at all. He wouldn't. He might think I'd take a fancy to them. I'm worried about your father'—his smile was gone now—'because your father is getting worried about RYNOX.'

'And a fat sauce,' said Peter, 'he's got. Worried about RYNOX. I'll scald his fat little ears! What d'you mean, F. X.—worried about RYNOX?'

She leant her elbow on the table and looked steadily, with a seriousness belying her words, into the eyes of F. X.

'Have a cigar, Tony?' said F. X. 'All right, Peter, I'm going to shoot in a minute. There's a maitre d'hotel with long pitchers just behind. Have a cigar, Tony, go on? . . . Look here, Peter, I don't know whether Tony's told you. Being Tony he probably has, but RYNOX is on about the stickiest patch of country we've ever struck. The position exactly is this—that *if* we can keep going for another six months, we shall be rolling along on top of the world, and right on top of the world. If we can't keep going for six months, we shall be rolling along somewhere in Lambeth gutter. Now, I'm not joking, Peter. I'm talking dead straight. RYNOX is mine. I mean, I started it, and I don't believe, for business purposes, in limited companies. A limited company means limited credit, and I like my credit hot, strong and unbounded. Hence the unlimited condition of RYNOX. But, Peter, do you know what an unlimited company means? It means that if the company fails, all the creditors can come down upon not only the company, but upon all the individual partners in the company. That is, upon me first, then Tony, and then your father. They can take not only the chairs and desks and pictures and carpets out of the office, but the tables and pianos and bath-taps out of *your house*.'

'All right, sir! All right!' Peter was smiling again now. A very different smile, a smile which made Tony gasp at his luck, and F. X. mentally raise a hat.

'All right, sir,' said Peter again. 'Yes, I knew that.'

A good lie; she hadn't known that. Both men knew that she hadn't known that. Both men if possible loved Peter more than they had five minutes ago.

'Your father,' said F. X., 'being, if I may say so, Peter, a very shrewd but rather timid Leadenhall Street business man, has frankly got the wind up. I keep soothing him down but I'd like you to help. I'd like you really to soothe him right down.' He turned to his son. 'Tony, has Sam said anything to you lately?'

'Sam,' said Tony. 'Sorry, Peter, *Daddy* thinks that if a man is under fifty he ought still to be playing with rattles. Sam doesn't understand me, I don't understand Sam. How on earth Peter ever managed to be—sorry, old thing! Anyway, in answer to your question, F. X. Benedik, Sam has *not* said anything to me. I think he has to Woolrich, though.'

F. X. laughed. 'If he said anything against RYNOX to Woolrich, I know what he'd get! That boy's keener on his job than anybody so fond of trips into the country's any right to be. RYNOX is graven on his liver.'

Tony moved the glasses from before him; leaned across the table; said in a different tone:

'Look here, Dad, we're going to pull this off, aren't we? Because if you think it's too much for you . . . but of course you don't!'

'I don't think anything,' said F. X. 'I know, boy, I know. By the way, did you see that friend of yours? Young Scott-Bushington?'

Tony's lip curled. 'I saw him all right. Cold feet though. Nothing doing, F. X.'

F. X. grinned. 'Don't look so solemn! That's all right. Look here, Peter'—he turned to the woman who was going to be his son's wife—'I don't know how much Tony tells you, but I'd tell you everything and then some. What RYNOX wants, Peter, is a hundred and seventy-five thousand pounds.'

'That *all*?' said Peter.

F. X. smiled. 'It sounds a lot of money, my dear, but in this sort of business it's, well, just nothing. You know what RYNOX are doing, don't you, Peter? RYNOX have practically chucked all their other interests into the fire to back the Paramata Synthetic Rubber Company.'

Peter nodded. 'Oh, yes, I know that. Tony does tell me things.'

'I expect,' said F. X., 'he does, and if I may say so, quite right, too. Well, the Paramata Synthetic Rubber Company's going—not west, but big. We've got the plant, we've got the stock, we've got the orders—some of them. We've got four big orders, Peter, hanging fire. They're coming along all right; they're German, three of them. But we've got to last out until they do come and then a bit, see? And that's what your father's worried about. He thinks we can't hang on, and I tell him we can. I tell him we've damn well got to! So you get at him, Peter, and tell him so, too.' He turned to his son. 'Tony!'

'Sergeant?'

'Paris for you, my lad. I want you to go and see Menier. If we don't recall that Valenciennes loan within the next six months we ought to be shot. I'd like it within a month. Just see what you can do, will you?'

Tony drew patterns upon the cloth with the haft of his fork. 'Right! Yes, I know Menier pretty well. We're rather pally, as a matter of fact. When do you want me to go?'

'Better take the five o'clock air mail. That gets you there in time for a full day tomorrow and Saturday and as much of Sunday as you'd like. Come back Monday morning . . .' F. X. looked at his son for a long moment. 'Stick at it, Tony. And by the way . . .'

Tony cocked an unobtrusive ear. He knew F. X.'s 'by-the-ways.' They generally concealed a major point.

'By the way,' said F. X., 'while you're with Menier, you might sound him. That Caporal group of his might put up fifty thousand. You could tell him six months and ten per cent, if you like. Anyway, try.'

Tony nodded. And at that moment the faces of father and son were so alike in every line that they might have been, not elder and younger brothers, but twins.

Peter looked at the watch upon her wrist. 'My dears,' she said, 'I must go. What about you? Or don't RYNOX do any work in the afternoon?'

F. X. stood up. 'They do. We've been chewing the rag here a bit too long as it is. Come on.'

They went on. Outside, father and son put Peter into a taxi; watched while the taxi purred out of Alsace Court and into the Strand.

F. X. turned to his son. 'Going back to the office, boy?'

Tony nodded. 'And you?'

F. X. shook his head. 'Not this afternoon. I'm going away to think.'

Tony waved a stick—they were half-way up the court by this time—at a taxi with its flag up. 'You have this?' he said. 'Or me?'

'You,' said F. X. 'I'm walking.'

The taxi came to a standstill abreast of them. Tony put a foot upon its running board and fingers to the handle of its door. 'Rynox House,' he said to the driver.

His father looked at him.

Tony opened the taxi door. He said over his shoulder:

'See you on Monday then.' He made to enter the cab.

'Tony!' said his father.

'Hullo!' Tony turned round; saw his father's outstretched hand; raised his eyebrows. 'Good Lord!' he said, but he took the hand. They shook; a firm grip, each as strong as the other.

'Do your best,' said his father, 'with Menier.'

Tony nodded and leapt into the cab and slammed the door. The engine churned. Tony looked out of the window. 'So long, F. X.,' he said.

'Good-bye!' said F. X., and raised his hand in salute.

COMMENT THE SECOND

ALL is not well with RYNOX. F. X. is probably not so confident even as his most pessimistic words to his son.

RYNOX is at that point where one injudicious move; one failure of judgment; one coincidental piece of bad luck, will wreck it. And it ought not—thinks F. X.—to be wrecked. For if it can struggle on for another six or seven months all his speculation, all his endeavour, will meet with incalculable success.

SEQUENCE THE THIRD

Friday, 29th March 193—   9 *a.m. to* 10 *a.m.*

F.X. sat at breakfast. Through the big French windows of his dining-room in William Pitt Street, the spring sun blazed, turning the comfortable but rather sombre room into a chamber of temporary glory. F.X., so to speak, read *The Morning Mercury* with one hand and with the other conversed with his man, Prout.

Prout was a short, stiff little man. There was a legend about Prout—started probably by F. X. himself—to the effect that he had nineteen hairs and that twelve of these were upon the right side of his parting and seven upon the other. He was clean-shaven—very shaven and very, very clean. He was also very quiet. There was another legend—this one having its birth with Tony—to the effect that Prout really was a 'foreigner,' only knowing three words of English: 'Very good, sir.' Prout, who had been with F. X. now for seven years—ever since RYNOX had been founded—adored F. X. In a lesser, quieter way he was fond of Tony. For Peter, he would have gone through nearly as much, if not quite, as for F. X. himself.

'If you, Prout,' said F. X., 'were Lord Otterburn and owned the daily paper with the largest net sale (don't forget net, Prout, there's always a lot of holes in a net) what would you do?'

Prout put a cover upon the dish of kidneys. 'Nothing, sir,' said Prout.

F. X. looked at him. 'And a very good answer too. Don't know what it is about you, Prout, but you always say the right thing with the most delightfully innocent air of not knowing you've said it.'

'Yes, sir,' said Prout. 'Excuse me, sir, but Mrs Fairburn wanted me to ask you whether you could see her for a moment before you leave for the office.'

F. X. nodded. 'Certainly, certainly.' He looked at his watch. 'You'd better tell her to come in now, hadn't you? I shall be off in a few minutes.'

'Very good, sir,' said Prout, and left the room so silently, so unobtrusively that the moment he was gone F. X. wondered, as he always wondered on these occasions, whether Prout had really ever been with him at all.

The door opened again. Mrs Fairburn came in. Mrs Fairburn was F. X.'s housekeeper. She, too, had been with F. X. for seven years. She, too, strictly within her very strict notions of right and wrong, would have done anything for F. X. She was, as Tony frequently said, almost too good to be true. Her hair, quite black despite her fifty-four years, was scraped from her forehead and piled high upon the back of her head. She wore black satin always. Sometimes there were bugles upon the black satin, but at other times the black satin was plain. Always when she walked the black satin rustled. About her severely corsetted waist was a belt and inevitably there dangled from this belt a bunch of keys. No one in the house had ever discovered—since nothing in this house ever was locked—what these keys were for. But always they were there, swinging and dangling and jangling. They told you, in fact, where Mrs Fairburn, moving about her duties in the tall, narrow house, could be found. You had only to stand still and listen. Presently you would hear them and then you could track Mrs Fairburn.

'Good-morning!' said F. X. 'Lovely morning, Mrs Fairburn.'

'Gord-mooning, Mr Baynedik. Truly a delaiteful day. It makes one feel really as if spring were drawing on.'

F. X. nodded. 'Yes, doesn't it? Well, what's the trouble, Mrs Fairburn?'

The thin lips of Mrs Fairburn writhed themselves into one of their sudden smiles. 'No *trouble*, Mr Baynedik. Nothing of the sort. Only rather an extraordinary thing has happened.' She produced, from some recess in the black-clad angularity of her presence, an envelope; advanced, bearing this rather like a lictor his symbolic bundle, towards the table. 'Mr Baynedik,' she said, 'this letter came by a district maysenger boy last night when you were out. It is, as you see, addressed to the housekeeper and staff. Seeing this address, Mr Baynedik, Ay opened the letter and inside Ay found three orchestra fauteuils for the Royal Theatre for tonight's performance. It is a piece which is apparently entitled *The Sixth Wife of Monsieur Paradoux* . . . rather, I must say, an astonishing title, Mr Baynedik.'

F. X. struggled with a smile. 'Certainly. Certainly. Damn silly names some of these people call their damn silly plays. Well, what about it, Mrs Fairburn? Do you want to go?'

'Ay did think, Mr Baynedik, that perhaps we would like to go as these seats have been presented to us so kindly, albeit so mysteriously.'

F. X. frowned. '*We'd* like to go . . . Oh, I see. You want to take the rest of the staff, Mrs Fairburn? Yes, take them by all means. Do you all good, I'm sure. And you can keep an eye on them and see that they don't get into mischief. Wonder who's sending you theatre tickets . . .'

'Ay cannot,' said Mrs Fairburn, 'understand the gift mayself, Mr Baynedik, but Ay believe there is a saying to the effect that one should not look at the mouth of a horse that has been given to one. Ay must confess that Ay could never see the meaning of this saying, but Ay have no doubt it is an apposite one.'

F. X. buried himself behind his paper. 'Yes. Go, by all means. It's very good of you, I'm sure, to chaperone the other two.'

'It was only,' said Mrs Fairburn, 'ewer dinner Ay was thinking of, Mr Baynedik. You see, if Ay go and also take the two gairls, there will be no one except Prout.'

F. X. crackled his paper. 'Prout'll look after me all right. He's done it before, you know. That's all right, Mrs Fairburn, you go.'

'Thank you, Mr Baynedik. Ay am sure that both Ay and the gairls are most grateful. Perhaps if you would not mind just casting your eye over these theatre tickets to ensure that we are not being made the victims of some cruel hoax . . .'

F. X. stretched out an arm from behind the paper. 'Let's have a look.'

With deliberation, Mrs Fairburn drew from her envelope three yellow slips.

F. X. took them and looked at them and grunted. 'Seem quite all right. I shouldn't worry about where they came from. As you say, a gift horse and all that. I expect it's some new advertising stunt or other. Get up to anything these people nowadays.' He thrust the tickets back upon their owner. 'Yes. Do all go. And by the way, Mrs Fairburn, as you go down perhaps you'd find Prout and ask him to come and see me. You leave me something cold tonight. I shan't want much. And Mr Anthony won't be in. He won't be back from Paris until Monday or Tuesday.'

Mrs Fairburn rustled out, to be replaced almost immediately by the silent Prout. F. X. looked at him.

'Well, Prout,' he said, 'Mrs Fairburn and the gairls are going out tonight. Very giddy! They'll leave me some food. You'd better get it ready.'

'Yes, sir,' said Prout. 'Very good, sir. At what time would you like to dine, sir?'

F. X. considered. 'Seven-thirty,' he said at last. He looked up at Prout's wooden visage and smiled. 'Don't worry, Prout. You'll be able to go round the corner to The Foxhound as usual.'

Prout was silent, but into his demeanour there crept the very faintest tinge of discomfort.

F. X. grinned at him. 'All right, Prout. Why shouldn't you go to The Foxhound? Good pub . . . I'll dine at seven-thirty then. I've got a business acquaintance coming to see me at ten, a Mr Marsh. When you've let him in, you can go out for an hour if you like.'

'Thank you, sir. Very good, sir. Shall I get the car, sir?'

'No. I'll walk to the office. Lovely day.' He stood up and folded his paper and threw it on to the breakfast table.

COMMENT THE THIRD

MRS Fairburn is going to the play. And so are the cook and the house-parlourmaid.

It is to be doubted whether Mrs Fairburn will approve of *The Sixth Wife of Monsieur Paradoux.* Cook certainly will and so, if she is not too nervous of Mrs Fairburn's rustling proximity, will Ellen.

It is unusual for complimentary tickets to be sent below-stairs. It is also unusual for housekeepers to associate voluntarily with the servants. But it is a long time since Mrs Fairburn has been to the Play.

And except for Prout, the house in William Pitt Street will be empty of anyone save its owner between the hours of seven-thirty and eleven-thirty.

SEQUENCE THE FOURTH

Friday, March 29th, 193—   11.30 *a.m. to* 12 *noon.*

Mr. Selsinger's gun shop in Vigo Street is very dark and very
low and very old, but it is—so many people will tell you—the
only place in the world in which to buy a gun. So, anyhow,
thought Peter (christened Petronella) Rickforth. Into the old
dark shop, whose walls are lined with wood and steel, Peter
brought, at half-past eleven that morning, some of the sunshine
which blazed upon all the rest of London.

Mr Selsinger himself, short and dapper and white-bearded,
came forward to serve her. Peter smiled at him. Mr Selsinger,
notoriously the most wooden-faced man between Bond and
Regent Streets, smiled back.

"Morning,' said Peter. She looked vaguely around her. 'I
want,' said Peter, 'to buy a gun.'

'Quite,' said Mr Selsinger.

'A gun,' said Peter again vaguely. And then, with a little burst
of confidence which made Mr Selsinger her slave for at least
so long as she should be within his shop: 'As a matter of fact,
it's a present for my fiance and d'you know, I tried and tried
to think of something that he wanted and then my future father-
in-law put me up to this. I expect you know him—Mr Benedik.'

'Mr F. X. Benedik.' Mr Selsinger smiled again; this time the
smile of the prosperous tradesman welcoming the friend of an
excellent customer. 'Certainly, madam. Mr F. X. Benedik has been
a customer and a very good customer of mine for a good number
of years.' Now Mr Selsinger put behind him, with one wave of
his slim white hand, the delights of social intercourse. 'May I
ask,' said Mr Selsinger, 'what sort of a gun you are requiring?'

Peter, who did not shoot, was vaguer yet. She said:

'I know nothing about guns, but I think it's a sporting gun I want. In fact, I know it is. Mr F. X. Benedik did tell me. He said . . . I've forgotten, d'you know.'

Mr Selsinger became helpful. He asked questions; many questions. At last he went to the rack labelled 'Three' and took from it a dully gleaming affair of blue steel and polished wood. 'If I might suggest it, madam, I think this is what you want. There is no better gun, if I may say so, in the world today.'

'It looks,' said Peter, refraining from holding out the hands into which Mr Selsinger so obviously wished to place his pet, 'perfectly lovely. I suppose it's a most frightful price?'

Mr Selsinger made a negative movement with his head. He also said something, but what the words were Peter did not hear. They were drowned by the storming entrance of another customer.

The low door swung open and crashed back—with a bang which ought to have and just did not break its plate glass against a show case. The bell, which the opening of the door set going, pealed angrily. A shuffling followed. Mr Selsinger stared. His white beard twitched with something very much like anger. Peter turned a head which strove not to seem too much interested.

The newcomer was a tall and somehow menacing figure. One didn't, Peter thought, notice his clothes but one did his hat. A black hat perched forward right over his face and its dark glasses. A soft black hat with a high crown pinched into a point. Beneath the dark glasses the grey moustaches and the little tuft of imperial seemed, not funny as many moustaches and beards seem funny, but extraordinarily—and, thought Peter, as she turned away, rather frighteningly—*important*. As he walked this man seemed to drag behind him his left leg. It did not bend, this leg, and it was carried so that its foot was broadside on to his progress. The inner side of the shoe, at each stride, scraped along the polished boarded floor with a little, hissing squeak most distressing to the ear.

Mr Selsinger, with a murmured word of apology to Peter,

went to the counter and leaned over it and touched something behind it. A bell pealed musically somewhere in dim hinter regions. Mr Selsinger then turned back, ignoring the newcomer, and began once more to expatiate upon the beauties of the gun now laid across the counter.

'It is, I can assure you, madam, a gun which any gentleman would very, very much appreciate, and it is the sort of gun, madam, which one need not be—if I may put it this way—ashamed of giving to a gentleman. However good a shot that gentleman may be, in fact, the better shot that gentleman may be the more strongly will he appreciate a first-class weapon like this. I have no hesitation, madam—'

What Mr Selsinger had no hesitation about was never to reach Peter's ears. Suddenly there came a roar from behind her. The newcomer was impatient.

'God blast it!' roared a raucous and somehow not English-seeming voice, 'God blast and blister it all! Am I going to get served or am I not?'

Mr Selsinger's neat little face, for one shocking instant, was sufficed with a lively glow. And then, with his return to decent, orderly, shopman pallor, came his superbly controlled voice.

'I am afraid,' said Mr Selsinger, facing the blank-eyed soulless stare of the stranger, 'that I, myself, am attending to this lady. I have rung the bell, as you doubtless heard. One of my assistants will very shortly attend to you.'

A scraping, thumping, squeaking as the stranger took four astonishingly rapid steps and now stood so close to Mr Selsinger that he almost touched him.

'I don't want,' said the stranger, and he spoke through his teeth, which were very white teeth, 'I don't want any of your damned assistants. What I want is a gun! Do you sell guns or don't you? Do you sell guns? Sell me a gun and be quick about it! Standing about here trying to look like the Pope of Rome. Twopenny ha'penny little tradesman. Can't understand what's the matter with this blasted city!'

There came from the back of the shop a young and hitherto confident assistant. Towards him Mr Selsinger waved a white hand.

'Mr Hopkins,' said Mr Selsinger, 'perhaps you would attend to this gentleman. He wishes . . . er . . . to make a purchase.'

The stranger exploded. 'Wishes to make a purchase, you little nincompoop! You bloody little half-wit!'

Mr Selsinger once more went pink from his eyes down to the edge of his neat white beard.

'You will pardon me, sir,' said Mr Selsinger stiffly, 'but your language . . .' One of Mr Selsinger's hands indicated in the most gentlemanly manner possible the presence of a lady. The stranger, stooping down from his height, thrust out his face until the dark glasses seemed to Mr Selsinger to be less than an inch from his own trim pince-nez.

'If,' said the stranger, and still he spoke without opening those startlingly white teeth, 'if you got on with your job and served me perhaps you wouldn't hear any language. I come into your damn shop and I wait about here minutes and minutes and then you send me a little poopstick like your boy friend Hopkins here. I want a *gun*, man!' Suddenly and most disconcertingly the stranger put back his head and laughed; a neighing mirthless sound which was described afterwards by Mr Selsinger as 'positively blood-curdling.'

'Guns,' said the stranger, 'guns! Little white maggots like you and your boy friend here selling guns! I don't suppose you've ever seen a peashooter fired in anger, either of you. You're both more like white rats than any man has a right to be.'

'Hopkins,' said Mr Selsinger, trembling with a mixture of rage and fear. 'Hopkins, will you please step into the street and see whether you can catch the eye of the constable.'

There was a clatter as the stranger's stick dropped to the wooden floor. For one triumphant moment, Mr Selsinger thought that he had conquered, but alas! the stranger was only laughing. The stranger was in a paroxysm. 'For God's sake,' he said, 'sell me a gun. I won't buy the cartridges here or I might blow your head off.'

It was at this point that Hopkins, a youth by no means so devoid of sense as his appearance would suggest, took matters into his own hands.

'Excuse me, sir,' said Hopkins briskly, 'what sort of a gun is it you're wanting?'

The tinted glasses of the stranger seemed to look him up and down.

'Heaven!' said the stranger, 'it speaks! . . . I want a nice, big forty-five colt with a rough grip if you've got it. Otherwise I'll have one of those heavy German automatics.'

Hopkins, talking rapid though very refined salesman talk, led the way to the far end of the shop. Mr Selsinger, his palms outspread almost on a level with his shoulders, his brows raised in terrific apology, turned to Peter.

'I cannot tell you, madam,' began Mr Selsinger, 'how deeply I regret . . . It is not often that in a quiet neighbourhood like this we—'

Peter cut him short. 'Really,' she said, 'it's quite all right. Please don't worry. And I'll have this gun. It's a beauty, I'm sure.'

Her voice, perhaps from a strongly repressed desire to laugh at Mr Selsinger and Mr Selsinger's distress, was both louder and higher pitched than usual. She said:

'I'll tell Mr Benedik how very kind you've—'

Once more an interruption. From where he stood beside Mr Hopkins, poring over a case of automatics and revolvers, the stranger swung round. 'Benedik!' he said. His voice was a harsh roar. '*Benedik!*' he said and laughed again. And if his laugh before had been a sound unpleasing, now it was ten times more so.

Even Peter—that most matter-of-fact and courageous young woman—felt the blood draining from her face.

Mr Selsinger fluttered helpless hands.

It was all over very soon. Back to the case of pistols the stranger swung. The stiff left leg seemed to trail behind its fellow on the turn. He pointed down to the case. 'I'll have that one,' he said.

Peter pulled herself together. 'If you would send the gun then to this address.' She gave a card into Mr Selsinger's trembling hands.

'Yes, madam. Certainly, madam. A pleasure.'

'And here,' said Peter, 'is one of my cards, if you would send the account to me.'

'Yes, madam. Certainly, madam.'

Peter, with one glance behind her, went out into the sunlit street. As the door closed behind her she was aware of a great, strangely disproportionate, relief.

COMMENT THE FOURTH

POOR Peter! An unpleasant experience at the time—but to turn out, in the light of the future, nothing less than tragedy.

SEQUENCE THE FIFTH

Friday, 29*th March*, 193—   7.30 *p.m. to* 10.20 *p.m.*

1

THE 'cold snack' foreshadowed by Mrs Fairburn turned, under the guidance of Prout, into a certainly cold but otherwise pleasing meal. Prout stayed in the room while F. X. ate. F. X. talked to Prout; seemed to extract from Prout's 'very good, sirs' and 'yes, sir—no sirs'—as, indeed, he well might—more solace than from many a so-called equal's conversation.

'Will you, sir,' said Prout, 'take coffee here or in the library?'

'In the library, I think,' said F. X. 'Just trot it along there as quick as you can, will you, Prout? I've got to run down to South Kensington to see Mr Rickforth.'

The coffee was drunk by 8.15, and by 8.20 F. X. was at the hall door.

'Will you, sir,' said Prout, 'be requiring a taxi?'

F. X. nodded. Prout, from some secret recess on his person, produced a large policeman's whistle. He ran down the steps into the road; blew three times, heartily; returned.

'Look here, Prout,' said F. X., standing on the topmost step. 'I'll be back as soon as I can, but there's someone coming to see me at ten. A man called Marsh. He's coming to talk business. If he should come here before I get back, just take him in, put him in the study, make the fire up, see that he has everything he wants—you know—then as I said, you can slip off to The Foxhound. I may be a few minutes late, but don't you wait in for me. Go and have your pint in comfort.'

'Yes, sir,' said Prout.

'Righto!' said F. X. He went down the steps just as a taxi

50

drew up at the kerb. 'Good-night, Prout, in case I don't see you again.'

'Good-night, sir. Thank you, sir.'

2

'Hups . . . I'm sure I beg your pardon. Don't know what it is about this spring weather, I'm sure, but it always seems to give me the same hups trouble. Well, dearie, I don't mind if I do—I think as I've got this hups trouble, I'll have a nice gin-an'-pep.'

'Mr Bliss! Mr Bliss! When you've finished talkin' to that young man about horse-racing, p'r'aps you wouldn't mind attending to me and Mrs Edwards . . . Thank you kindly *I'm* sure! Mrs Edwards is going to take a large gin with a very small—now, mind you, Mr Bliss, only a very small—dash of pep. Is that right, dear?'

'Yes, hups, thank you. Pardon, Mr Bliss! My error!'

'And as fer me, Mr Bliss, I'm sticking to the old-and-mild. Don't know 'ow it is, but some'ow that seems to suit me best.'

Mrs Edwards, her gin with its dash of pep clasped firmly in her right hand, sank back again upon her chair. She looked at her friend and momentary chairwoman, Mrs Welbee. Mrs Welbee was fumbling for coins in a well-worn but not too well-stocked purse.

Behind the bar, the magnificently stout and rosy-cheeked Horace Bliss waited patiently.

'Hups!' said Mrs Edwards from her chair. 'Very quiet tonight, hups, aren't you, Mr Bliss hups? You'll pardon me!'

Bliss rubbed his hands together and rested them upon the beer-slopped counter. 'Oh, I don't know, Mrs Edwards. Never very busy this time of the evening. I've no doubt you'll see a little company before long. Either some of the old faces or some new ones . . . That's one thing about my trade, Mrs Edwards, one's always seeing new faces and strange new characters.'

'Personhups'ly,' said Mrs Edwards from her chair, 'I must say, Mr Bliss, that I prefers the old comhupsrades, if you know what I mean. I like to see the old hups faces.'

'Well, well, Mrs Edwards, each man to his taste, as the French say.'

'Them French,' said Mrs Welbee doubtfully, 'they'd say anythink! All the same, dear, I must say's I could do with the sight of a fresh face in this 'ere bar. I comes in night after night and I get fair sick of the same old faces. Most of 'em puts me in mind—present comp'ny always excepted, dear—of one song of old Marie Lloyd's. "One of the ruins that Cromwell knocked abaht a bit." Ow, Gawd save us! Wot's this?'

'*Hups!*' said Mrs Edwards.

Mrs Welbee slid further along the oaken settle; leaned over to her friend. 'That's where Bliss gets all these French sayings. I'll lay *'e's* no Englishman.'

The newcomer was a tall and burly man. His left leg was stiff, and seemed to trail him as he walked. Dark glasses hid his eyes and always his head was out-thrust as if striving for better sight. Upon his head was a strange black hat, high and pointed. He had grey fierce moustaches and a little block of grey beard. His face seemed deeply tanned. As he walked, dragging the stiff leg behind him, up to the bar, he muttered ceaselessly to himself, and with each muttering came a flash of white teeth in the dark face.

'Can't say,' said Mrs Welbee, 'that I likes the looks of '*im!*'

'Nor me neither, dear.'

The newcomer rapped upon the bar with a florin drawn from his pocket. 'Brandy!' he said in a queer, hoarse voice, and then when no server was immediately forthcoming, the word 'Brandy!' again. This time the word was shouted.

Bliss came through the curtained alcove from the public bar. He looked with disapproval upon the author of this noise. He said:

'Now, now! No shouting, *if* you please. I'm not a bird, I can't be in two places at once. Now I *am* 'ere, p'r'aps you'll tell me what I can get for you.'

The stranger leaned both hands on the counter, palms downward. He bent over with his face out-thrust towards Bliss. He said with a low-controlled snarl: 'You heard me! Brandy, I said!'

Bliss's rosy cheeks grew a shade paler. There was, he decided, something 'uncommon nasty-seeming' about this customer. *Uncommon nasty-seeming.* He turned to his shelf, took down from it a bottle of brandy and a glass. 'And 'ow much brandy would you be wanting, sir?' His tone was noticeably more civil.

'Fill it up!' said the hoarse voice.

'I beg pardon?' said Bliss.

Once more that forward movement of the head. Once more the hissing, deliberate repetition:

'Fill it up, I said!'

Mr Bliss filled it up. He kept hold of the glass with his right hand. He said:

'That'll be five shillings.'

The stranger plunged his hand into his trouser's pocket; threw down upon the bar a handful of silver. Some of the coins rolled to fall near the feet of Mrs Edwards. Wheezing, she bent to pick them up. The stranger, his back to her, took no notice. He raised the glass of brandy, looked at the light through it, put it to his lips and with one twist of of his wrist sent the three-quarter tumblerful down his throat. Bliss watched him with goggle eyes.

He set the glass down; he turned. Mrs Edwards was still grovelling. She had in her palm now two half-crowns, a shilling and a sixpence. There was more, it seemed, to come. The stranger made for the door. The inner edge of the shoe upon the foot of the injured leg hissed raspingly over the floor.

Bliss came to life. Just as the stranger's hand was on the door, Bliss realised what Mrs Edwards was doing.

'*Hi!*' called Bliss, 'just a minute, sir!' His tone was sharp and eager. It apparently had something in it which startled the stranger, who whipped round with an agility amazing in one of his condition—whipped round, at the same time flashing his right hand towards his hip pocket.

'What's that?' It was more snarl than voice.

'All right, sir. All right!' Bliss backed away until a sharp crack on the back of his head told him that he had reached his limit and could back no further. 'All right, sir!' he said again, holding out a hand. 'If you like to drop money about and then not claim it, that's your funeral. And what're you doing with your 'and in that pocket, anyway?'

'Ha!' The stranger laughed; a sound, as Mrs Edwards was to say later when describing this amazing event, 'enough to freeze the hupsmarrow in a body's bones.'

The stranger laughed again, but he took his hand from that hip pocket. He turned his glance—that blank, black glance—upon the two women in the corner. Mrs Welbee clutched at Mrs Edwards. 'Ow, my Gawd!' said Mrs Welbee under her breath. 'Ow, hups!' said Mrs Edwards.

'That money,' said the stranger, in a soft wheezing voice, 'you can keep it. If you drink with that money, the drink will probably choke you.'

He swung back again to face the still staring, still petrified Bliss. He said: 'You! Can you direct me—I am a stranger to London'—they noticed here for the second time what trouble he had with his r's. He seemed to say them right down in his throat—'can you direct me to William Pitt Street, Mayfair?'

Bliss shook his head. 'Don't know the neighbour'ood. Don't know the neighbour'ood. Don't know the neighbour'ood.'

'Parrot!' said the stranger. Again the scraping noise as that lame leg trailed after him, and then a little eddying draught as with his going the swing-door swung once or twice backwards and forwards.

Bliss stared at the door. 'Well, I'm damned!' he said.

'Well,' said Mrs Edwards, 'may you say so!'

3

F. X. stood before the fire in Rickforth's study. He shook his head. 'No, Sam, no!' he said. 'I won't come in. In the first place I haven't changed, in the second place I don't feel much like a party tonight.'

'Oh, be a man, F. X.! Might just as well. Be a man!'

'Sammie,' said F. X. 'The picture of you telling someone to be a man is almost more than I can bear. No, I'm going, old son. Just that little chat to straighten up the Carruthers-Blackstone matter was all I wanted. No, I won't have another drink and no, no, no, I won't come to your party.'

'Shall I tell Jevons to get you a taxi?'

'Sam, you can keep your taxi. I'm going to walk; a lovely night like this. No, I'm going to walk quietly home and when I get home I'm going to have my interview with Mr Marsh.'

Rickforth looked puzzled. 'Marsh?' he said. 'Marsh?—oh, isn't he the fellow who's always writing you letters and ringing you up and all that sort of thing? I got him on the 'phone the other day. Wouldn't seem to take no for an answer.'

F. X. nodded. 'When you say nuisance, Sam, you understate the case. That fellow's a swarm of locusts. He's a public blight.'

He began to move towards the door. Rickforth came with him. 'What's he after exactly?' he said. 'This man Marsh, I mean?'

F. X. laughed; a laugh with, in it, perhaps a little less than his usual humour. He said:

'What's he after? Didn't I ever tell you, Sam?'

'Good Lord!' said Rickforth, 'I remember. Yes, he's the man that thinks he was the inventor of the Paramata recipe. Knew you in South America or something.'

'That's the boy!' said F. X. 'Still, he's been pestering me for the last year now. I'm going to settle with him tonight.'

Rickforth looked shocked. 'You're not going to pay him any money?'

F. X. grinned. 'Pay him hell! As a matter of fact, I'm going to offer him £25 or a kick out. I think he'll take the twenty-five quid. He's one of those hard cases with a soft-boiled inside. Well, I must push along, Sam. Good-night.'

Rickforth saw him to the door. 'Sure I can't get you a taxi?' he called after him on the steps.

On the pavement F. X. paused. 'Not on your life,' he said. 'I'm walking.'

'Good-night, then!' said Rickforth.

'So long, Sam!' said F. X., and raised his stick in salute.

4

Prout, sitting comfortably behind the *Evening News* in the library's biggest chair, shot suddenly to his feet. A frown—an indignant frown—suddenly creased his usually expressionless face. What I mean, thought Prout, it's all very well to *knock*; it's all very well to *ring* . . .

Before he had got half-way down the hall to answer this knocking and ringing, it came again, and if the first knocking and ringing had been excessive in their loudness, they had been as nothing to this second assault.

Prout broke into a run. Really, he couldn't have this! He put his fingers to the door-handle and remembered, as he did so, that this was probably Mr Marsh . . .

If it was Mr Marsh, thought Prout, all he could say was that Mr Marsh was a very odd and a very nasty, dangerous-looking sort of customer. What with them dark spectacles and that little bit of beard and that funny black hat, to say nothing of the way that leg of his seemed to trail round after him as if it didn't belong somehow . . . Well! . . .

'Good-evening, sir!' said Prout.

'Marsh,' said a harsh grating voice. 'My name's Marsh. Benedik in?'

'Mr Benedik,' said Prout, 'is out, sir. For the moment only.

Mr Benedik left word, sir, that if you was to come by any mischance before he got back that I was to ask you to step inside and make yourself comfortable while you were waiting. He will not, in any case, keep you waiting more than a very few minutes.'

A sound which Prout could only liken to the growl of a dog was his reply. Prout led the way through the hall and then down the passage to the study. After him, trailing the lame leg with a little scraping sound upon the carpet, came the visitor. He still kept on his pointed black hat. Prout stood aside. The visitor passed in. To the visitor's back Prout said:

'Is there anything I could get you, sir? . . .'

'All you can do for me,' said the visitor without turning, 'is to take yourself off out of it. It's Benedik I want.'

'If you would care, sir,' said Prout with considerable dignity, 'for a whisky and soda, you will find syphon, decanter and glasses on the table there.'

The face of the visitor turned round to peer at him. The voice of the visitor said:

'I may wear dark glasses but I'm not blind.'

'Very good, sir,' said Prout, and withdrew. He shut the door.

For a few minutes he dallied, awaiting his master's return, and then, knowing his master and remembering his master's instructions, he put on his cap, put pipe and tobacco into his pockets and set out for The Foxhound and its saloon bar. The front door of No. 4 William Pitt Street closed softly behind him.

COMMENT THE FIFTH

It is to be hoped that Benedik will not allow himself to be
unduly troubled by Marsh. At this very critical stage in Rynox's
affairs it is essential that the head of Rynox should keep only
the business before his mind.

Somehow RYNOX must weather the next six months.

SEQUENCE THE SIXTH

EVERY police constable carries a Big Four beard in his pocket. Some police constables, realising this, do nothing about it; others, realising this, do far too much. Neither class achieves the beard. Others neither miss opportunities nor try to make opportunities. They, of course, do not get the beard either, but they do at least go some way towards earning it.

Of this kind, the not pushing but equally not backward type, was BL. 413, Ernest Henry Lawrence.

Lawrence's beat lay across Mayfair from India Court on the west to William Pitt Street on the east. At 10.20 p.m. exactly Lawrence was half-way between the two extremes of his beat. That is to say, he was in the centre of Shepherds' Market. He had been on duty for an hour and during that hour nothing at all had happened. Lawrence was thinking to himself, now for a quiet night, and then Lawrence suddenly stiffened. He had heard sounds which he knew—he was a man of quick ear and ready intelligence—to be revolver shots. And not one revolver shot, but a fusillade of revolver shots . . .

Lawrence began to run. Despite his uniform, which he had often thought must have been specially designed to prevent quick movement, he made very creditable pace. He had only memory to guide him, for after that outburst silence had fallen again upon the neighbourhood. He came out of Goss Street into William Pitt Street which runs across it at right-angles. At the junction he stopped. His ear and memory combined could tell him no more. But Lawrence was in luck. There came to his ear the sound of running feet. He wheeled round to face the runner. It was, perhaps fortunately for the runner, a man whom

59

he knew. It was, in fact, Arthur Wiggin, the potman of The Foxhound.

'Hi!' said Arthur Wiggin as soon as he saw the uniform. 'Hi!' He came pelting up. He peered for a moment. 'It's you, Harry, is it! Thank God! Here, boy, there's something for you. 'Ear that barrage just now?'

Lawrence nodded. 'I did. What d'ye know?'

'Number four,' said Arthur Wiggin. 'Number four, boy! That's where it come from. Up this way!' They began to run side by side. As they ran:

'See anything?' asked Lawrence.

'Nary a thing. Heard plenty, though! There you are, boy, that's four. What you goin' to do?'

'Get in, you cuckoo! Here, you assist the Law! You go up to the front door and kick up hell's delight until somebody answers. I'm going round the back.'

Lawrence put his hand to the locked iron gate which leads down between Nos. 4 and 5 to the communal garden at the back; put his hand upon the gate and vaulted it—helmet, dragging coat, lumbering boots, and all. He knew the geography of these houses, did Lawrence. In a moment he had reached the back door of No. 4; had smashed his fist through the pantry window, unlatched it and was half-way in. As he scrambled, sucking at a bleeding fist, across the darkness of a scullery between the kitchen door and the pantry, he heard the beginnings of Arthur Wiggin's assault at the front.

Lawrence found switches and pressed them down. The basement was flooded with light. He tore up the basement stairs.

'Hi!' yelled Lawrence. 'Hi! Anybody about? Hi, there!'

Only the echoes of his own voice came back to him. The house was quiet; dead quiet. Lawrence went more slowly. He slipped out his truncheon, wrapping its thongs about his fingers in the proper style. He came out at the top of the servants' stairs. 'Hi!' he yelled again.

Once more, only echo.

Lawrence did not smoke. He had therefore a keen nose. There came to his nostrils suddenly the acrid tang of gunpowder smoke. It was drifting towards him from the passage on his left. He switched on the passage light and run down the passage. There was one door at the end of the passage. It was shut but it was not locked. He opened the door, he went in, arm and truncheon above his head; one never knew . . .

There was only one person in the room, and that a dead man. He lay with his body face downwards across the window sill of the one open window. The sill supported him just below his breastbone. His legs sagged hideously. His left arm was out of the window; his right hung down inside the room, in its tightly clenched fingers a revolver. There was a telephone upon the big writing table. Lawrence used it, reporting to his station. Having reported, he went back to the body. Without moving it he managed to see that this was Mr Benedik, whom quite well he knew by sight.

'Tck!' said Lawrence, clicking his tongue against the roof of his mouth.

Mr Benedik had been shot through the head. The bullet had entered—it must have been fired at closeish range, thought Lawrence—just over the right eye. It had come out just behind the left ear.

'Tck-tck!' said Lawrence again. He went and stood by the writing table. He took off his helmet and laid it down. His eyes searched the room. They saw, in two of the walls, the marks of bullets—seven in all. The holes upon the eastern wall were much bigger than the holes upon the western wall. Lawrence's eye left the bullet holes; travelled about the room. Suddenly they widened. On a chair drawn up in front of the fire, lay a man's hat; a black hat of a peculiar shape; a soft black felt hat with a soft crown pinched up high into a point. Gingerly, using the brass fire-tongs to do it, Lawrence picked up the hat. Inside the brim in ink was written 'B. MARSH.' He put the hat back where he had found it; replaced the tongs.

He went back to the body, knelt down and looked at the revolver so tightly clasped in the dead hand. He knew a little of firearms, enough to see that this was the gun which had made the smaller bullet holes.

Lawrence spoke to himself. 'Reg'lar jool,' he said. 'That's what it was!' He shook his head sadly as he climbed to his feet. F. X. had been, as he was with everybody, popular with Lawrence . . .

END OF REEL ONE

REEL TWO

1

(TELEGRAM from Petronella Rickforth to Anthony X. Benedik. Handed in at 1 a.m. Saturday, 30th March, 193—)

BENEDIK HOTEL POMPADOUR BOULEVARD MARAT PARIS
RETURN IMMEDIATELY GRAVE ACCIDENT F. X. TERRIBLE
NEWS PLEASE COME PETER.

2

(Letter from Magnays Bank Limited to Messrs. Rynox, dated 30th March, 193—)

DEAR SIRS,—I am to express the deep and sincere regret of my directors and myself at the tragic demise of Mr F. X. Benedik.

I have, I fear, also to state, in regard to the A. and B. Accounts of your firm, that it is unfortunately impossible for me to allow any further drawings until those accounts are placed upon a sounder basis.

With respect to the C. Account this, as you know, (*vide* my letter of the 27th instant) has been closed as regards any further drawings.

So soon, of course, as one or more of the accounts is placed upon a credit basis, we shall be only too glad, not only to permit drawings upon that account, but to consider the possibility of re-opening accommodation upon the other accounts.

In the meantime, however, I fear that my directors will not countenance any applications for further accommodation, that already granted to your firm being considerably in excess of the usual.

Yours faithfully,

ALBERT PERCIVAL HERRING,
Manager.

3

(Letter from the Midland and Capital Bank Limited, Lombard Street, to Messrs. Rynox, dated 30th March, 193—)

DEAR SIRS,—I have the painful duty of expressing the very sincere regrets of my directors and myself at the tragic and untimely end of Mr F. X. Benedik.

I have also to state, on the explicit instructions of my directors, that it is unfortunately impossible for the bank to allow any further increase in the overdraft with which your firm is at present being accommodated.

The directors hope that they will see, within a few days, the substantial reduction which was personally promised—by Mr F. X. Benedik himself—a few days ago.

Yours faithfully,

MAURICE HIPLAM.
Manager.

4

(Letter from The Arcade and General Finance Corporation to Messrs Rynox, dated 30th March, 193—.)

DEAR SIRS,—We note that the last interest payment on our loan (B4124) to you on the 27th February last is still unpaid.

We would ask you to take immediate steps to meet this. Failing your satisfactory reply within this week, we shall—though we are, in the present painful circumstances, most reluctant to adopt such a course—be compelled to place the matter in other hands.

Yours faithfully,

DOUGLAS IAN MACFARLANE,

Director.

5

(Departmental Report by Detective Inspector F. Wellesley, C.I.D., 1st April, 193—.)*

Subject.	F. X. Benedix, deceased.
Place.	4 William Pitt Street, W1.
Time.	Approx. 10.30 p.m.

Proceeded to William Pitt Street as above, on Superintendent Fox's instructions, at midnight on Friday, the 29th ult. Found there, Police Sergeant (BL. 342) Humphreys and Police Constable (BL. 413) Lawrence. Copy of Sergeant Humphreys's report is attached at A together with a copy of

Plans Constable Lawrence's Preliminary Report (A. 1.)
Attached. Attached at B is a plan of the study at No. 4 William Pitt Street and at B. 1. the ground floor plan of the house and garden.

---

* It is not necessary to give copies of all the purely routine and merely repetitive reports, etc., attached to D.-I. Wellesley's report. The plans, however, as being of use to the reader, are given at the end of the report.

Position
of
Body.

The body of deceased had not been moved when I arrived. It was lying face downwards across the sill of the window (marked X on Plan B). The head and shoulders were out of the window and also the left arm. The right arm was hanging down inside the room; in the hand a small five-chambered .44 Colt revolver. From this revolver four shots had been fired.

Cause
of Death.

Deceased had been shot through the head, bullet entering above the right eyebrow and coming out behind the left ear, at short range, bullet inflicting this wound being from a heavy Mauser automatic pistol. Deceased had obviously been shot from just outside the window as he leant out. Bullet was found embedded in the western wall of the study midway between the end of the fireplace and the junction of the western and northern walls (marked A). This bullet has been submitted to Professor High who gives it as his considered opinion that it is undoubtedly the one which caused death.

Bullets
Found
in Room.

Other bullets (nine in all) were found in the room. Three of these were from the Colt revolver in the dead man's hand and six from the Mauser pistol. The six Mauser bullets (this is excluding, of course, the one which caused death) were embedded in the eastern wall of the study where it forms a party-wall to the passage leading from the hall. The three bullets from the Colt were found grouped together in the angle made by the junction of the western and northern walls.

Mauser
Automatic
Pistol.

I found a Mauser automatic, recently fired and with its magazine empty, in the shrubbery which lies on the far side of the path from the house. (See Z on Plan B.) The markings on the Mauser bullets found (including that which caused death) corresponded with the rifling of this pistol. Professor High is prepared to state on oath that they were fired from this pistol.

Enquiries show that this Mauser pistol was purchased from Selsinger & Co., Vigo Street, W1 on the morning of Friday the 29th ult.

Colt Revolver. The Colt revolver found in deceased's hand was known by the household to have been in his possession for many years.

Hat. In a chair (see Y on Plan B) was found a black hat of the 'sombrero' variety. Inside the band is written *B. Marsh.*

Summary of Statements Taken P.C. (BL. 413) LAWRENCE heard several shots while on beat and running up William Pitt Street, met:

(Wiggin) ARTHUR WIGGIN, Potman at Foxhound Public House.

Wiggin was returning from an errand and walking out of William Pitt Street when he heard the shots and guessed, from their direction, that they were proceeding from No. 4.

(Prout) WILLIAM PROUT, manservant to deceased.

Prout stated that deceased dined at 7.30 p.m. on Friday and then went out stating destination to be house of Samuel Rickforth of No. 18 Consort Gardens, South Kensington.

Deceased, Prout states, left instructions to the effect that a Mr Marsh was going to call at about 10 p.m. and that if he (deceased) were not back when Marsh called, Marsh was to be admitted and left in the study. Prout states also that deceased gave him permission to go out so soon as Marsh should have been admitted, as he (deceased) would not be more than a few minutes after Marsh.

Prout states that at 10.10 he admitted a man who stated his name was Marsh. He wore the hat subsequently found in the study.

Prout's description of Marsh is: tall, heavy build, grey moustache and imperial beard, dark glasses, peculiar limp with left leg which he seemed 'to drag after him.' P. can't say as to clothes except hat but it is definite that the clothes were not evening dress but a 'dark suit.' States Marsh's manner violent and hectoring.

Five minutes after admitting Marsh, Prout left the house and proceeded to Foxhound P. H. in Shepherds' Market. Remained there until closing time at 11 p.m. (this statement substantiated by numerous witnesses) when returned to 4 William Pitt Street to find Sergeant Humphreys in charge.

(*Fairburn*)   ELSA VICTORIA FAIRBURN (Widow), House-keeper of deceased.

Fairburn, accompanied by the other two female servants (see below) left the house at 7.30 p.m. to proceed to the Royal Theatre for the evening performance. Returned home with aforesaid companions at 11.20.

Fairburn states that upon Thursday evening the 28th ult. a letter was brought to the house by a District Messenger Boy, this being addressed to 'Housekeeper and Staff, 4 William Pitt Street.' She opened it and found that it contained three back stall seats for Friday evening's performance at the Royal Theatre. Nothing else was in the envelope. Across the corner of the tickets, Fairburn states (and this evidence is corroborated by the other two servants) was written in pencil in printed characters 'Compliments.' Fairburn states (corroborated by Prout) that she told deceased on Friday morning the 29th ult, of this incident and received his permission to go to the theatre taking the servants. She has no idea at all of where the tickets could have come from. She also states that she mentioned the 'mysterious origin' of the present to deccased and he, too, was mystified but thought 'it was part of a publicity campaign.'

Fairburn had been housekeeper to deceased for seven years.

(*Briggs*)   SARAH JUBILEE BRIGGS, Cook to deceased.

Corroborates evidence of Fairburn.

Briggs had been in the employ of deceased for two years.

(*Watson*)   VIOLET DORIS EMMELINE WATSON, House-parlourmaid to deceased.

Corroborates as above. Watson had been in deceased's service for eighteen months.

(*Rickforth*)   SAMUEL FARADAY RICKFORTH, Partner in deceased's business, Rynox.

States that at approx. 9 o'clock on Friday evening, the 29th ult., deceased called to see him on a business point. They discussed the point and deceased, refusing to join a party which was going on at that time in Mr Rickforth's house, left, stating he must get home as he was expecting a visitor, such visitor being a man named Marsh. (*N.B.* The name found in the band of the sombrero hat dropped in deceased's study.)

Questioned as to his knowledge of Marsh, Mr Rickforth states that he had not personally come into contact with Marsh. He knew, however, that

Marsh was a one-time acquaintance of Mr Benedik's. They were together in South America during some part of the period 1911–1913. Mr Rickforth had frequently heard deceased speak of Marsh who, deceased stated, was a madman who imagined himself the real inventor of the Synthetic Rubber process (Paramata Synthetic Rubber Co.) which has lately been the main concern of the firm Rynox.

Mr Rickforth further stated that Marsh was always writing letters to deceased both at his home and his office and frequently telephoning for appointments. Upon one occasion Marsh visited the office of Rynox without an appointment and created a disturbance. None of the partners (deceased, Mr Rickforth, or Mr Anthony X. Benedik) was in and eventually deceased's secretary, Christabel Pagan, had to have Marsh threatened with ejection by Commissionaires.

Mr Rickforth further stated that after telling him of Marsh's intended visit to his house that night deceased added some words to this effect: 'For the past two or three years he's been worrying my life out. I'm going to settle with him.' Deceased, Mr Rickforth states, then added that he intended to make Marsh an offer of a small payment for the sake of getting rid of him: if Marsh did not take the payment, then matters would have to take the ordinary course.

Questioned further, Mr Rickforth stated that deceased had never even hinted at the possibility of personal violence from Marsh.

(*Pagan*)   CHRISTABEL PAGAN, Secretary of deceased.

States that she knew of the appointment at 10 p.m. at William Pitt Street with Marsh as she heard deceased making this over the telephone. Marsh had twice already rung up that morning. Corroborates *re* Marsh's letters, telephone calls and visit. States that deceased never seemed more than very much annoyed over Marsh's pestering; certainly never gave any hint that Marsh might be dangerous.

Showed to me file of letters (two specimens attached at C 1 and 2)—(whole file available if necessary) from Marsh. The address on all letters except four in the file is: Pond Cottage, Little Ockleton, Surrey (see later statement by George Hillman). The other four bear no address.

Miss Pagan's description of Marsh's appearance tallies with that given above by Prout. She also states that his manner was 'frightening and very snarling'; curious inflection to voice; guttural r's; walked with a dragging limp of left leg.

(*Woolrich*) BASIL WOOLRICH, Secretary and Treasurer to Rynox.

States he heard deceased once or twice make mention of a man, Marsh, who was pestering him. Had also heard some mention of the incident (see above) when Marsh called at the office. Had never thought much about this matter. Could not help further.

(*Musgrove*) LESLIE MUSGROVE, Box Office Clerk, Royal Theatre.

States that on the morning of Thursday the 28th ult. sold three stalls (J. 15, 16 and 17)—the numbers sent to Fairburn and staff at No. 4 William Pitt Street (see above) to what he describes as a 'queer character.' No name was given, of course, during the transaction. Musgrove's description of the purchaser of the tickets tallies exactly with the description above. States the man was 'very rough-mannered and had a domineering way of talking. Rather foreign-looking. Used plenty of bad language.'

(*Butters*)   EMANUEL BUTTERS, Manager, Crofton Street Branch, District Messenger Service.

States that at 12.15 p.m. on Thursday last the 28th ult. he was given a letter addressed to the housekeeper and staff, No. 4 William Pitt Street, and was asked to have this letter delivered between 6.30 p.m. and 6.45 p.m. Instructions were most explicit. According to Butters (corroborated by two boys) this letter was handed in by 'a big man with a limp. Very excitable and violent in his ways.' His further description tallies with that given above. Butters also states that the man made 'quite a scene' until he was definitely promised that the letter should be delivered exactly within the times he mentioned.

(*Selsinger*)   CHARLES BYRON SELSINGER, Gunsmith. States that at approximately 11.40 a.m. on Friday last the 29th ult. a strange customer came into his Vigo Street shop and purchased a Mauser automatic pistol. (This pistol he subsequently identified as the pistol I found—see above—dropped in the shrubbery outside the window of the study at No. 4 William Pitt Street.)

Selsinger states that the customer who made this purchase was eccentric and violent in his ways. Among other offences, he used foul language in front of a lady client. At one time, he (Selsinger) asked his assistant to fetch a constable but withdrew this command on the purchase being completed. Selsinger's description of the purchaser of the Mauser agrees in detail with that given by other witnesses of Marsh. States that he was most offensive in speech and most alarming in behaviour. Walked with a sinister and peculiar dragging limp. States also that the name of the lady customer in the shop at the time was Miss Rickforth. (This is a peculiar coincidence.)

(*Hopkins*)   FRANK ALBERT HOPKINS, Assistant to Selsinger.

Corroborates Selsinger's evidence down to last detail.

(*Miss Rickforth*)   PETRONELLA RICKFORTH, daughter of Samuel Rickforth, Partner in Rynox Ltd.

Corroborates evidence of Selsinger and Hopkins and adds that she thought the man not only dangerous but insane.

(*Hillman*)   GEORGE HILLMAN, of Pond End Farm, Great Ockleton.

States that a Boswell Marsh rented Pond Cottage, Little Ockleton, from him on a year's lease, the transaction taking place on the 3rd September last. States knew nothing personally of his tenant except what he saw of him at the interview. Describes him as a 'big, queer-like, foreign sort.' When asked, agreed with the description of Marsh given above. States also that he received several minor complaints, but being 'an easy-going sort of chap,' had never taken these up, not living in Little Ockleton and rarely going there. Knew nothing else. States that he had no reference from Marsh and didn't consider this necessary as the whole amount for the yearly tenancy was paid by Marsh at the time the lease was signed. It was not paid by cheque but in notes.

General Opinion of Marsh—Little Ockleton District.

Bears out all previous evidence to show that

Marsh was eccentric in behaviour as well as appearance. Cordially detested by all villagers. Varied tales of threatened violence towards men and children.

(*Chigwell*) SARAH CHIGWELL, Charwoman employed by Mr Marsh.

States that she was never frightened of Mr Marsh. Also states that, except to pay her and give her instructions, he never spoke to her. Also states (statement corroborated by various as above) that Marsh did not use Pond Cottage more than a few days in each month. Nearly always his visits were over weekends although on more than a few occasions he came down for a night in midweek. Description of Marsh tallies with all those above. In further description of Marsh without a hat, states that his hair was 'black with a lot of grey about it.' Could not state colour of eyes as never saw Marsh without spectacles.

(*Benedik*) ANTHONY XAVIER BENEDIK, son of deceased.

States he was in Paris from Friday evening last until Saturday morning at 2 a.m. when re-called by his fiancée, Miss Rickforth (see above). States had heard his father frequently mention Marsh but had never paid any serious attention to the possibility of Marsh's being dangerous. Knew nothing of Marsh and had never seen him. Had once spoken to him over the telephone. No further help possible.

(This concludes the testimony of the persons interviewed to this stage.)

(*Summary*) BOSWELL MARSH, having, by correspondence and telephonic and personal message extending over the past six months, expressed the opinion that he had been unfairly treated by deceased, obtained on Friday the 29th ult. an interview with deceased. He and deceased were alone in the house. The interview commenced at approximately 10.15 p.m. At approximately 10.30 p.m. P.C. (BL. 413) Lawrence heard a repeated succession of shots from the neighbourhood of William Pitt Street and, upon investigation, made the discovery of deceased's body. In the room was a hat which bore Marsh's name and was habitually worn by Marsh. In the shrubbery across the path immediately beneath the open window of the room was a Mauser pistol purchased that morning by a person answering exactly to the description of Marsh.

The house was empty because the manservant, as usual, had been given permission to go out between ten and eleven; because Mr Anthony X. Benedik, son of deceased, was in Paris; and because the housekeeper and two female servants had gone to the theatre, the tickets for the theatre having been presented to them anonymously, the anonymous buyer being a person whose description tallies exactly with that of Marsh.

Marsh, as the evidence collected will show, bore, or thought he bore, a definite and bitter grudge against deceased.

Deceased was lying half in and half out of the window. In his right hand was his own revolver from which three shots had been fired. Deceased had been shot through the head by a bullet from the automatic pistol bought that morning by the man whose description tallies with Marsh's.

Documentary evidence—specimen letters attached and also extracts, attached at D, from deceased's diary—shows that Marsh, for some years, had imagined himself (rightly or wrongly) to be a victim of sharp practice on the part of deceased. *(N.B.*—It will be noted that this documentary evidence of Marsh's ill-will begins as early as 1912—see extracts from deceased's diary covering the period 1912 to the present year referring to interviews and letters with Marsh to the number of at least four a year. See also specimens of recent letters from Marsh. These letters begin, as will be seen, when Marsh arrived in England six months ago.)

(Conclusions)   *Concluded* that deceased was shot by Boswell Marsh at the end of the interview commencing at approximately 10.15 p.m. on the night of Friday, March 29th, 193— such shooting being the result of an interview at which Marsh sought to obtain redress for imaginary or real grievance against deceased. There seems no doubt that the interview began stormily and ended with the threatening of deceased by Marsh with his automatic pistol. Deceased must, atop of this threatening, have produced his own revolver; whereupon shots must have been exchanged and Marsh, having jumped out of the open window, must have turned and, seeing deceased leaning out after him, gun in hand, must have fired the last shot, which killed deceased. Marsh then must have run straight across the gardens, in his fright dropping the pistol (see Point Z on Plan B) and made exit by one of the passages upon the other side of the gardens, *i.e.* passages between the houses in Fox Street. The ground being very hard, he left no footprints, but his way of exit must have been as suggested. (The fact of Marsh's

having been frightened out before actually killing deceased is borne out to my mind by the finding of his hat within the room. If he had gone after killing deceased, he would not have left his hat as testimony against himself.

(*Action*)   Every effort is being made to trace the present whereabouts of Marsh. Warrant for Marsh's arrest is made out and held pending discovery.

F. WELLESLEY, D.-I.

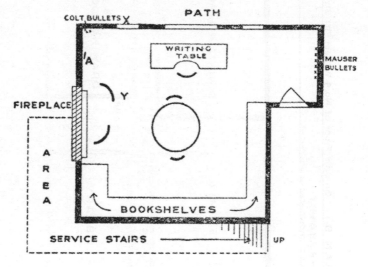

PLAN. B. Study of No. 4 William Pitt Street.

■ Z

SHRUBBERY

PATH

COLT BULLETS X

A

WRITING TABLE

MAUSER BULLETS

Y

FIREPLACE

AREA

BOOKSHELVES

SERVICE STAIRS ⟶ UP

X = Position of body.
A = Position of bullet which caused death.
Y = Chair in which sombrero hat was found.
Z = Point where Mauser Pistol was found.

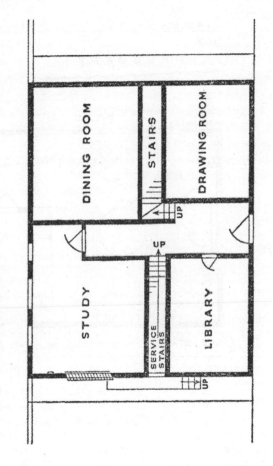

PLAN. B.1. Ground Floor of No. 4 William Pitt Street.

SHRUBBERY

DINING ROOM

STAIRS

DRAWING ROOM

STUDY

LIBRARY

SERVICE STAIRS

UP

UP

UP

6

(Letter from Messrs Rynox to Magnay's Bank Ltd., dated 1st April, 193—.)

DEAR SIRS,—In reply to yours of the 30th ultimo, I have to express the gratitude of my Directors for your kind expressions of condolence concerning the tragic end of our senior partner, Mr Francis X. Benedik.

I have to inform you with respect to the remainder of your letter under reply that by the end of this week the firm will be placing upon a credit basis both the A and B accounts, paying £12,750 into the A account and £17,312 17s. 3d. into the B account.

Yours faithfully,
(for Rynox)
BASIL WOOLRICH,
(*Secretary and Treasurer*).

7

(Letter from Messrs Rynox to Midland and Capital Bank Ltd, Lombard Street, dated 1 April 1930—.)

DEAR SIRS,—In reply to yours of the 30th ultimo, I have to express the gratitude of my Directors for the expressions of condolence concerning the tragic end of our senior partner, Mr F. X. Benedik.

I have to inform you with respect to the remainder of your letter under reply that by the end of this week the reduction of our overdraft promised by by Mr F. X. Benedik (£7000) will be made.

When this sum has been paid into the account I shall

be glad if you will favour me with an interview at your earliest convenience.

> Yours faithfully,
> (for Rynox)
> BASIL WOOLRICH,
> (*Secretary and Treasurer*).

8

(Letter from Messrs Rynox to the Arcade and General Financing Corporation, dated 1 April 193—.)

DEAR SIRS,—Your letter of the 30th ultimo: I send you herewith this firm's cheque, dated for the 7th inst., for £279 13s. 11d., being the last interest payment on our loan (B. 4124).

> Yours faithfully,
> (for Rynox)
> BASIL WOOLRICH,
> (*Secretary and Treasurer*).

9

(Letter from Basil Woolrich to Hugh Gleason, dated 1st April, 193—.)

PRIVATE AND CONFIDENTIAL.

DEAR GLEASON,—Don't worry about Rynox. It's all right. Our accounts not only with your firm but with our brokers and others will be settled within a short period—ten days at the outside.

I'd be much obliged and so would A. X. Benedik if you would do what you can to counteract the rumours which are going round about the firm's insolvency. I think you would find it would be not only to your own but to everybody's advantage if you could work along these lines for us.

Perhaps you could meet me for lunch tomorrow at the usual place.

Yours sincerely,
BASIL WOOLRICH.

10

(Memorandum from Anthony Xavier Benedik to Basil Woolrich, marked CONFIDENTIAL, dated 1st April, 193—.)

Hope you have written Banks, Arcade, and Gleason as arranged. Rickforth fixed. He won't trouble us just yet awhile. When he comes back he may be more reasonable. Destroy this.

11

(Letter from Naval, Military and Cosmopolitan Assurance Corporation to Anthony Xavier Benedik, dated 1st April, 193—.)

DEAR SIR,—
    Policy No. HI.32. Francis Xavier Benedik, decd.
    We have to acknowledge receipt of your letter of today's date containing claim for payment of £277,777, the amount for which Francis Xavier Benedik, deceased, was insured with this Corporation.

The matter is receiving the attention of the President himself and you will hear from us within a short while. We trust that you will appreciate that the unusual and very tragic circumstances of Mr F. X. Benedik's death, coupled with the unusually large sum assured, put the matter outside mere routine.

I am, Sir,

Yours faithfully,

(for Naval, Military and Cosmopolitan Assurance Corporation),

E. THURSTON MITCHELL,

(*Vice-President*).

12

(Letter from Rynox to Grey Friars Trust Ltd, dated 2nd April, 193—.)

DEAR SIRS,—In reply to your letters of the 28th, 29th, and 30th ulto., and your telephone messages of yesterday, I have to inform you that I have now discussed the situation with Mr Anthony X. Benedik.

Mr Rickforth, to whom your letter is addressed, is at present in the country suffering from a nervous breakdown brought on by the terrible shock of the news of Mr F. X. Benedik's tragic end.

Mr Anthony Benedik, on behalf of the firm, empowers me to state that the balance of our debt to you (£3254) over our joint deal in the matter of Rampole's, Ltd. will be paid to you within the next few days.

Mr Anthony X. Benedik also wishes me to state that if necessary he will meet you over this matter. He is, however, very busy and trusts that this letter will serve the same purpose as an interview. The latest date for payment would be ten days from today, but in all probability the payment will be made some little time before that.

Yours faithfully
(for Rynox),
BASIL WOOLRICH.
(*Secretary and Treasurer*).

13

(Letter from Fielder, Puckeridge, Fielder and Fielder, Enquiry Agents, to Naval, Military and Cosmopolitan Assurance Corporation, dated 2nd April, 193—.)

DEAR SIRS,—
Policy HI. 32. Francis Xavier Benedik deceased.
Further in *re* yours 30th ult. Our agents have now covered whole field of enquiry. Attached is our report plus résumé of Police Report kindly lent by Scotland House. From this you will see that there is no doubt as to cause of death, deceased having been undoubtedly shot by Boswell Marsh. Police now searching for Marsh but so far unsuccessfully. Think they must get him within a day or two.
Considered opinion: Claim lies; Corporation liable for full amount of Policy, £277,777.
(For Fielder, Puckeridge, Fielder & Fielder,

A. K. MIMRAM.

14

(Letter from Petronella Rickforth to Anthony Xavier Benedik, dated 3rd April, 193—.)

DARLING,—I hope you are having my medals struck. In regard to ribbons for same, please consult yours faithfully as I don't trust your eye.

I know you didn't think I could do it, but I've done it. I am, you know, rather an extraordinary young woman. As soon as I got your note on Monday I tackled Samuel, going to the office to do it. I'm sorry to say that I found him, although he is my father, in a most deplorable condition of pure funk. To tell you the truth, Tony, I hadn't quite believed you until the sight and sound of him made me realise that it was true. If I'd been a creditor of RYNOX I'd have tried to get whatever it is they do—Petition filed, isn't it?—just after one glimpse of him.

It was very funny really. When I walked in he tried to shoo me out like a hen shooing its young. But I wasn't to be shoon. As a matter of fact, I went into the room and locked the door. And then I told him what you told me on Sunday night. I pointed out to him that you and Woolrich were quite undoubtedly the stuff. I told him that, equally undoubtedly, be wasn't. I told him that no Rickforth should ever show such blue toes. I told him that if he'd only come away from that office and give it a chance under you and Woolrich, the whole thing would come so straight that in a very little while he'd be even more opulent than he had been. I asked him what he thought, F. X. . . .—Oh, Tony, darling, isn't it dreadful? He was so utterly dear!

To go back to Samuel, however, I told him this, I told him that, and I told him several sorts of the other. All to no purpose. All he could say, when I kept ramming your name and your excellence and your F. X.-ishness down his throat—all he could say was (you know, Tony, I'm almost ashamed to tell you this, but, poor old fellow, he's never been in a school where they develop guts) that *he was surprised that after what had happened you could give your mind to the office!*

I'm afraid that finished me, or perhaps I should say glad. Anyway, I suddenly became the complete Cassandra, or whoever the lady was who was always very clever. I pretended to crack. I pretended to give way to parental and superior knowledge. I said that of course he must know best now I came to think about it. I was very, very sad. I was very, very unhappy. I was very, very frightened. I left the office and went home.

When he came back in the evening—I suppose you and Woolrich managed to keep him from doing anything too utterly silly during the day—when he came back I was absolutely prostrate. I was having a real, double-barrelled, super A quality nervous breakdown. I couldn't stand London—no, not for one minute longer could I stand London. I wept and shuddered and started at little noises. Most convincing performance. It brought out all the man in Samuel. Asked what had best be done for her, the maiden replied, 'Take me, father, to the country! Take me away from—all this!'

Samuel, driving the Sunbeam himself (poor old fellow, the maiden couldn't bear the thought of anyone else being in the car except her father) took me away from all that. We went to where we are now. You know my best time, Tony—an hour and ten minutes. Samuel took four and a half! Ye Gods! it was terrible. The nervous breakdown was almost genuine at the end. We hurtled through the night at well over twenty. Every time a rabbit looked out of a hedge we stopped. Every time a lorry pulled out across us we went on!

But we got here—I think the time was about 3.75 g.m.— and we went to bed, having found, to Samuel's horror and my apparent dismay, that Kate was not there as she should have been but paying a visit to that mother of hers who will never die. (Please note, dear sir, that Kate's absence was due to the machiavellianism—is that spelt right?—of our Miss Rickforth who, by telephone, presented Kate with a holiday.) Now read what our special correspondent has to say:

STRANGE MYSTERY in SURREY WEEKEND COTTAGE.
Prominent Business Man Loses Understandings.

Our frightfully special correspondent writes:
'Mr Samuel Rickforth, a prominent Director of Rynox, is held a prisoner in his charming and palatial country residence on Hindhead. Mr Rickforth, the best of fathers, had, although pressed and hedged about by the cares of business, himself driven his daughter, that well-known and extraordinarily beautiful young leader of Hammersmith society, down to the country on the previous night.

'On arriving at his country residence (chming view, 45 mins. stn., Co's water c; unusual offices); Mr Rickforth was horrified to find that the whole of the extensive staff had absented themselves without leave. He therefore took over the duties of housekeeper, cook and nurse and tenderly put Miss Petronella Rickforth to bed. Then, exhausted, he himself retired.

'On waking next morning with the lark at approximately 10.30 a.m. Mr Rickforth leapt from his bed, intending to attire himself and then to see to Miss Petronella's wants, obtain attention for her, and proceed immediately, driving his high-powered car, back to London and work.

'Imagine Mr Rickforth's dismay when he found that not only had the trousers of the clothes he had been wearing the night before had disappeared but that also there was not, so far as he could find, another pair of these far from decorative but almost essential garments in the house.

'In something very much like panic and a dressing-gown, Mr Rickforth hurried along the numerous and softly-carpeted passages to the room of Miss Petronella Rickforth. Miss Petronella Rickforth seemed a good deal improved in health. She could not, however, throw any light at all on the mystery of the missing leg-wear.

'*Later*. Mr Rickforth still without trousers.

'*Later still*. Mr Rickforth, for fear of sciatica, sitting up in bed swearing, and reading *Pilgrim's Progress*.

'*Later than ever*. Mr Rickforth, with Napoleonic flash of insight, decides to telephone for trousers, but is horrified to find that the telephone is cut off.

'*Too late*. Mr Rickforth, having conducted a hunger strike for some time in protest at Miss Petronella's most unfilial refusal to do anything about trousers and having rejected harshly her offer of a brassiere (almost new) and a pair of cami-bockers, breaks down and descends to the charming dining-room with its outlook over the Surrey hills in order to eat the by no means despicable meal prepared by Miss Petronella's own fair hands.'

Seriously, darling, after twelve hours of this I began to get the wind up. After all, one never knows what a parent will do if driven far enough. After all, thank the Lord, it's all come out all right. He really is, when he can get over himself, rather an old dear. He's given me his parole that he won't go back to London until told. And I have given him back one pair of trousers. I have, however, cut a piece out of the seat so that he can't go out of doors.

If you can, do come down and see me. I shouldn't come in in case he has a suspicion—most unjust I'm sure, Mr Benedik—that the scheme has been anything to do with you. Just pull up in the lane outside and hoot about four times.

Do come if you can, dear, I'm longing to see you. If you were anyone but you, I should say I hope you don't think the rather idiotic tone of this letter shows that I'm not feeling for you and for myself. As you're you, I'm not going to trouble to say it.

Do come as soon as you can, but if you can't I shall understand.

Bless you!
PETER.

15

(Extract dated 4th April from official shorthand record of Coroner's inquest held on the body of Francis Xavier Benedik. Coroner, Doctor Ongle. Extract is from Dr Ongle's summing up, but also contains the jury's verdict.)

... And so, gentlemen, I think you will not find any other course open to you than to fix upon this man, Boswell Marsh, as the person directly responsible for the shooting of the deceased. You have listened to the chain of evidence, which proves that Marsh was a man of violent and unpleasant nature, imagining himself wronged by the deceased. You have seen, too, documentary evidence supporting this. You have seen and read the very full diary left by the deceased, covering the last twenty years of his life, and from that have gathered that right from their first acquaintance in South America in 1911 Marsh and the deceased were at loggerheads. You have had it conclusively proved to you that Marsh visited the house in William Pitt Street on the night of deceased's death and that the pistol found, dropped by Marsh in his flight, had been purchased by Marsh that morning. You will have seen, from the evidence, the subterfuge employed by Marsh to ensure that the housekeeper and two female servants should be absent from the house that night, and you will assume that Marsh had sufficient knowledge of the ways of that house to know that the manservant, too, would be absent at the time of the arranged appointment.

These are just a few points which come to me as afterthoughts. I do not think, gentlemen, that there is anything else which I need say. You will now please consider and confer if necessary, and then let me have your verdict . . .

Mr Coroner, I have consulted with the jury and I find that there is no need for us to retire. Our verdict is one of murder against Boswell Marsh.

16

(Letter from Naval, Military and Cosmopolitan Assurance Corporation to Anthony Xavier Benedik, dated 7th April 193—.)

DEAR SIR,—
   Policy HI. 32. Francis Xavier Benedik, deceased.
   Further to our previous communication and also to the interview which our President had with you yesterday, I have pleasure in enclosing herewith the Corporation's cheque for £277,777 (Two Hundred and Seventy-seven Thousand, Seven Hundred and Seventy-seven Pounds).
                    I am, Sir,
                         Yours faithfully,
                              MARADICK FOWLER,
                                   (*Treasurer*).

17

(Memorandum from Chief Commissioner of Police, Major-General the Earl of Styng, K.C.B., D.S.O., M.V.O., C.I.E., etc., to Superintendent Shanter, dated 19th April, 193—.)

Benedik.

I note your report on this case. It is highly unsatisfactory. The preliminary investigations seem to have been conducted with intelligence, but the work of the Department after the preliminaries seems puerile.

Benedik was shot on the 29th of last month. Three weeks have elapsed. There is no doubt whatsoever that the murderer was Boswell Marsh, and Marsh has not been taken. Why? A man of such distinctive appearance cannot easily hide himself. The ports have been watched, and all his usual places of resort, and yet you have not got him.

I expect to hear of his arrest within the next ten days.

STYNG.

18

(Memoranda covering period April 29th to May 31st, 193—.)

From Chief Commissioner to Superintendent Shanter.
BOSWELL MARSH.
Please report. STYNG.

From Superintendent Shanter to Chief Commissioner.
BOSWELL MARSH
Regret have no further progress to report.
T. SHANTER, Supt.

From Chief Commissioner to Superintendent Shanter.
BOSWELL MARSH.
Ref. my memorandum of last week. Please report.
STYNG.

From Superintendent Shanter to Chief Commissioner.
BOSWELL MARSH.
Much regret Department has no further information yet
to hand in regard to the above.
T. SHANTER, Supt.

From Chief Commissioner to Superintendent Shanter.
BOSWELL MARSH.
Reference previous correspondence and our meeting of
Tuesday, have new steps produced any information
regarding whereabouts of Marsh?
STYNG.

From Superintendent Shanter to Chief Commissioner.
BOSWELL MARSH.
Much regret new steps produced so far nothing further
re above.

SHANTER, Supt.

19

(Extract from Minutes of Chief Commissioner's weekly meeting
with Superintendents, Scotland Yard, dated July 2nd 193—.)

17634. DECIDED that Standing Item No. 4—Boswell Marsh—
shall in future be deleted from the agenda, no further
progress or information having been forthcoming.
Matter to be raised at every sixth meeting.

REEL THREE

SEQUENCE THE FIRST

1st October 193—   1.30–2.30 *p.m.*

1

THE restaurant of Monsieur Isidor Laplanche is in Dover Street. Its small and neat exterior gives to the unsuspecting client who tries it for the first time no indication either of the excellence of Monsieur Laplanche's food, wines and cooking, nor of the preposterous charges made by Monsieur Laplanche. Monsieur Laplanche started the Restaurant Pyrénées in the middle of May of this year, 193—, exactly five months before the date with which this Sequence deals.

Peter Rickforth had never happened before this day to enter the Restaurant Pyrénées. She did so now. As usual, Peter was late. As usual, Tony waited for her. With Tony was Peter's father a Samuel Rickforth even pinker, even plumper, even—though this may seem impossible—more prosperous seeming than when we last saw him. Tony, save perhaps for an increased likeness to F. X., is unchanged.

Peter, as she comes through the swing door held deferentially open by a gigantic Nubian who looks like the King of Abyssinia but really comes from Agamemnon, Ill., and, strangely enough, is proud of it, seems changed only in that she is, incredibly, even easier to look at.

Tony looked at his watch.

'It is,' said Peter, coming up to them, 'absolutely useless . . . Hullo, Parent! If you will wear waistcoats like that I don't think you ought to put chains across them . . . It's absolutely useless, Tony, to do that tongue-clicking, watch-gazing stuff with me.'

'I know,' said Tony, to his betrothed, 'I know. But I shall always do it. Have a drink?'

Samuel Rickforth shook his head. 'No, no, not here. That table's been waiting twenty minutes now, and I don't think, my dear,'—he took his daughter's arm—'you can know Laplanche's chef. If you did, you wouldn't suggest any more delay.'

They went out of the lounge and through the centre swing doors and were in the small saloon. They sat at a round table in a window which was frosted up to the half of its height to prevent, so Peter suggested, Monsieur Laplanche's customers from seeing the felinities of Monsieur Laplanche's larder. Peter tasted the soup of the chef of Monsieur Laplanche. Peter approved. She approved continuously throughout the luncheon. This, seeing the size of the bill which her father would have very shortly to pay, was fortunate for her father's peace of mind.

'And how,' said Peter over her coffee, 'is business? No, I'm not asking you, Parent. They never tell you anything, you know. You get all the "Yours of the 5th to hand" and "is receiving our earnest attention" stuff. I'm talking to Anthony Xavier.'

'Business,' said Tony, 'is big. Or just about to be big.'

'My dear boy!' Samuel Rickforth was aghast. 'Just about to be, you say! It *is*! It *is*!'

'That's nothing,' said Tony, 'to what it's going to be. It's going to be so BIG in about another three months that what it is now will look like two-penn'-orth of cold gin by comparison.'

Peter leaned forward, holding out a white hand. 'Give me another cigarette,' she said. And then, 'Serious?'

Tony looked at her. Their eyes met. He nodded. 'Stone cold serious,' he said. He looked at Rickforth. 'This morning,' he said slowly, 'we heard from Hamburg and Brisbane. Both cables confirmed the orders.'

Samuel Rickforth's glass, luckily with only a small puddle of wine at its bottom, dropped from Samuel Rickforth's fingers. Samuel Rickforth stared.

'God bless my soul!' he said at last. '. . . you don't mean it, my boy?'

'I never,' said Tony, 'say anything I don't mean.'

'Except,' said Peter, 'when you mean to.'

'God *bless* my soul!' said Samuel Rickforth again.

'Hamburg,' said Peter, 'sounds like sausages. Brisbane sounds like I can't think what. Am I to take it that Hamburg and Brisbane . . .'

'If you,' said her betrothed rudely, 'didn't talk quite so much, you'd hear a lot more.'

'Ha!' Samuel Rickford exploded. 'Quite right, my boy, quite right!'

Peter looked at her father sternly. 'Trousers!' she said.

Samuel Rickforth winced and endeavoured to cover his wincing with a jovial laugh and failed quite signally.

Peter looked once more at Tony. She said:

'And will Hamburg and Brisbane make you so busy that you won't have time to remember that we're supposed to be getting married at the end of next month?'

'I shouldn't,' said Tony, 'think so. I tell you what, I'll ask Woolrich if he'll give me leave.'

Peter's eyes blazed. 'As much as mention that man's name to me, young Benedik, and I'll . . .'

'Now, now!' said her father. 'What's the matter with Woolrich, anyhow? I must admit that when Tony wanted to make him a partner I wasn't altogether in favour of it, but since he's been one, I must say I've had an even higher opinion of his capabilities than I had before.'

'His capabilities,' said Peter, 'are, thank Heaven, nothing to do with me. I do not like thee, Doctor Fell . . . And nor do you, Tony.'

Tony shrugged. 'Whether I like him or not don't matter two hoots. As a matter of fact I don't mind the fellow at all. Still a bit too fond of slipping off to the country, but then he always was. I remember the Guv'nor used to pull his leg about it. The Guv'nor'—Tony's face as he spoke now was so reminiscent of F. X. that even Samuel Rickforth opened unimaginative eyes—'stood it, though, and Woolrich wasn't a partner then, and if F. X. stood for a man taking day's holidays every now and then without asking until he came back, well, you can bet that man's a good man. And Woolrich is a good man. That Brisbane show's entirely his.'

'Wool me no more riches,' said Peter. 'I don't like him. I don't like him. I don't like him. If you grasp my meaning, I don't like him. The conversation having thus been tactfully changed, I will ask you, Xavier—now I'm being quite serious, darling—exactly why Frankfurt and Melbourne—sorry! Sorry! Whatever the places are—why they make such a *tremendous* difference.'

Tony looked at her. His grey eyes softened. He knew his Peter. He said:

'All right, I'll tell you. They're going to make this big difference not only because they're big orders in themselves for Paramata, but because of what they'll lead to. At Brisbane that new motor-tyre centre's starting. It's the nucleus of what's going to be in a few years almost Australia's biggest productive enterprise. And Brisbane are doing that on us, as you might say. And an order from Hamburg means, you can bet your boots, twenty other orders, most of them bigger, from other parts of Europe. RYNOX is straight now, and has been for quite a while. It's even been making money—all out of Paramata—but, Peter, the money it *has* been making is going to look like Little Leonard's Post-Office Savings Book ... Yes, absolutely! I mean it!' He knocked the ash off his cigar and got to his feet, a tall and heavy but lightly moving and graceful figure.

Peter looked up at him. 'Going?' she said.

He leaned on the table and looked down at her, giving a slight and sidelong glance at Samuel Rickforth. 'Yes,' he said.

'RYNOX never sleeps. Come with me; you'll be able to see your friend Woolrich.'

'I think,' Peter said, 'that I almost dislike you . . . Good-bye, darling.'

Comment the First

RYNOX has recovered; RYNOX is upon the edge of Big Things. But the edge of Big Things is a narrow edge. And narrow edges are slippery. If any trouble—even such as may be caused by malicious rumours—were to come to RYNOX now, before the edge of Big Things had become a plateau, RYNOX would be in for such a fall that every bone in its body would be broken.

RYNOX may not know it, but RYNOX must be careful and very careful.

SEQUENCE THE SECOND

October 2nd, 193—   12 *p.m.* to 5 *p.m.*

1

To Basil Woolrich, sitting in the room at the top of Rynox House which had used to be that of F. X., came the clerk Harris. Harris, who had knocked four times and then, getting no answer, had taken his courage in both hands and entered, walked over the thick-piled carpet to the big table in the window. To Harris's eye there presented itself only the smooth, golden poll of the junior partner. Harris coughed.

'Excuse me, sir,' said Harris.

Woolrich looked up. In these last months of hard work much of the tan had faded from his face. A deep frown had carved permanent lines between his brows. The corners of the well-cut mouth were perpetually downdrawn.

'Excuse me, sir,' said Harris, 'but there's a gentleman in the outer office . . .'

'Most,' said Woolrich, 'extraordinary!' Then sharply: 'Well! What of it?'

Harris smiled dutifully at the dubious joke.

'It's only, sir, that . . .' he said, 'well, to tell you the truth, sir, we can't get rid of him. Says he's got very important business with the firm. Won't see anyone except yourself or Mr Benedik. We've tried all ways, sir, but we can't get him to state his business or to go. As a matter of fact'—Harris's tone grew eager—'I was wondering whether you would think it best if I got Fred and Fred and I were to . . .'

For a moment Woolrich smiled, and the flash of white teeth seemed momentarily to take ten years from his age. He said:

'No, I don't think so, Harris. What's his name?'

With something of the air of an apprentice and diffident member of the Maskelyne family, Harris produced a card. He laid it upon the blotter of the junior partner.

'James?' said Woolrich, 'Captain James? Never heard of him.'

He picked the card up and examined it. A cheap affair, printed, and recently printed, for with his thumb nail Woolrich succeeded in blurring the capital C of Captain. The card bore no address; no club; nothing save those two words: CAPTAIN JAMES.

Woolrich dropped from his fingers the little piece of pasteboard, which lay, now face downwards, upon his blotter. Woolrich looked at Harris. Woolrich said:

'What's he look like?'

Harris put his head upon one side; considered a moment.

'A toughish lot, sir,' he said, after a pause, 'very toughish. Looks as if he'd just come back from some tropical country, sir, and there he is, sitting in a chair between Miss Pagan's desk and mine looking as if it would take a charge of dynamite to shift him.' Harris grew eloquent. 'Like some sort of heathen idol, sir. He's sitting there; he's not saying anything, sir; he's not *doing* anything. He's just sitting there staring across the room and every time we say anything to him he just repeats like some unholy sort of parrot: "I want to see Mr Benedik and if Mr Benedik's not here, I want to see one of the other partners."'

Woolrich rose from his chair and stretched himself; walked over to the window and stood a moment looking out. Harris waited, shuffling his feet silently this way and that on the thick carpet.

Woolrich swung round at last. 'All right,' he said. 'Shove him along, Harris.'

The face of Harris became three o's—eyes and mouth—of interrogation; aghast interrogation.

'You don't mean to say, sir . . .' Harris began.

'I said, Harris, fetch him along.' Woolrich's tone was once more that coldly official, perfectly courteous and yet offensive tone for which most of the staff so cordially detested him. Harris muttered apology in his throat and was gone.

Woolrich went slowly back to his table and picked up the card and looked at it. He threw it down and sat. As he reached out to his ash-tray to crush out a stub which had for some time nearly been burning his fingers, there came another rap on the door.

'Captain James, sir,' said Harris.

Woolrich rose. A tall, beautifully built and easily graceful figure. He was even taller than F. X. or Anthony. His face wore the wooden mask of gravity with which the ordinary English business man will meet any caller the nature of whose call is unannounced beforehand.

Harris, leaving himself upon the outer side, shut the door with a soft click. The newcomer crossed the room towards Woolrich. He was, this Captain James, a short and thick and extraordinarily solid-seeming man. While his height could not have been an inch more than five-feet six, his weight, and all good hard weight by the look of it, must have been nearer fourteen than thirteen stone. His gait was rolling, but somehow with the roll neither of horses nor the sea but rather a mixture of both. He was clean-shaven. His face, which was a square, mahogany-coloured and uneven slab, had eyes in it which seemed to be set almost midway down its length; very small eyes of a curious faded blue whose whites were white no longer, but an even, angry crimson. His clothes were an old and faded suit, double-breasted, of the kind which one immediately associates, for no known reason, with pilots.

Woolrich looked at him.

'Good-afternoon,' said Woolrich.

Captain James smiled, revealing a jagged and irregular set of tobacco-coloured teeth. With Captain James, there came towards Woolrich a miasma of Holland's Gin.

'I'm very pleased,' said Captain James, 'to make your acquaintance.' His voice was just the sort of voice which Woolrich imagined would proceed from that mouth and body—a deep booming sound somehow out of tune.

Woolrich pointed to a chair. 'Sit down, won't you?'

'I don't mind,' said Captain James, 'if I do.' He sat, placing, one upon each knee, square, short-fingered, powerful hands whose backs were matted with a thatching of black hair.

Woolrich remained standing. He looked with disfavour—disfavour which he did not endeavour to conceal—upon his visitor. But his visitor went on smiling and his visitor's eyes went on steadfastly holding Woolrich's gaze. Woolrich, looking away, sat himself down behind his table.

'If you wouldn't mind,' he said, 'stating your business as quickly and briefly as you can . . .'

The smile of Captain James disappeared and suddenly Captain James's face became, most improbably, like the face of a vulture.

'My business,' said Captain James, 'is with the other partner, Benedik.'

Woolrich got to his feet. 'In that case . . .' he said, coldly.

'One moment, one moment!' said Captain James. 'And not so much of the smooth stuff, either. I am seeing you, Mr Woolsack, because I want to make quite sure that I *do* see this Benedik. I want your assurance that I *will* see this Benedik.'

'I fail to see'—Woolrich's tone was now in itself an insult—'how I can ensure you an interview with Mr Benedik if I don't know what your business is with Mr Benedik.'

'Isn't that,' said Captain James in tones of admiration, 'said pretty!' Once more his square lipless mouth opened to show the discoloured fangs. 'But I'm not here for that sort of stuff, Mr Woolsack. I'm here on *business*. And very, very important business!' Suddenly Captain James leaned forward and raised his right hand from his right knee and pointed with stubby, vast forefinger at his host. 'See here, Mr Woolsack,' said

Captain James, 'this Rynox is a big concern, isn't it? This Rynox, from all they tell me, is going to be a lot bigger. But suppose this Rynox was to get a nasty smack in the eye! How about that? Suppose a story was to start round about Rynox—a nasty story, Mr Woolsack. How about that, eh? I'm just showing you how important my business is . . . A nasty story . . . and nasty stuff happening to Rynox and about Rynox just now . . . Well, that'd just about put Rynox in the ditch, wouldn't it now?'

Woolrich rose. 'If this is a sample of your business conversation, I think the sooner we put an end to it the better.'

'Ve-ry smooth!' said Captain James. 'It's a gift, that's what it is. But it doesn't go down with me. Not on your life it doesn't. And you can push all your pretty little buttons for all I care and bring in all your damn'd little clerks. *They* won't stay here very long.'

'If this,' said Woolrich, 'wasn't faintly humorous, it would be quite impossible.'

'If you,' said Captain James, 'would get a large canvas bag and push it right down your neck, that'd be better. I want to see Mr Benedik and I'm *going* to see Mr Benedik, and when I *have* seen Mr Benedik you'll laugh the other side of that pussy face of yours. Just look at me a minute.'

Woolrich looked at Captain James. Suddenly it was borne in upon Woolrich that Captain James was in earnest.

'All I can do,' said Woolrich, 'is to mention your visit to Mr Benedik. Whether he sees you or not is his own affair. If you'd tell me something of your business I might be able to be more useful. As it is, I can't.'

Captain James got to his feet, a process which looked as if it ought to take, by reason of his amazing solidity, much longer than actually it did.

'I am,' said Captain James with a leer, 'much obliged to you, Mr Woolsack. I shall be more obliged to you when I've seen this Benedik. My address, at the moment, is Croft's Hotel,

Milady Street, Strand. 'Phone number . . . that's right, Mister, write it down . . . 'phone number, Strand 1234. And don't forget, Mister, that see him I've got to or . . .'

Woolrich was pale. Woolrich was not used to this sort of thing. But Woolrich did his best. He said:

'I can hardly think that that tone will do you any good. If I might give you a warning, it certainly wouldn't pay with Mr Benedik himself.'

Captain James smiled. His small and bloodshot eyes were not touched by the smile.

Woolrich pressed one of the row of bells upon his desk and in answer there came, not Charles, who was elsewhere, but Harris the clerk . . .

Woolrich, alone, stood by the window staring out over the tops of many houses . . .

Down the corridor towards the outer office and the lift Captain James rolled in the wake of Harris. Harris arrived at the end of the passage and held open the swing door which let out on the corridor and stairs. But Captain James did not pass through the swing door. Captain James halted and eyed Harris up and down in a way which made Harris acutely discomfortable.

'Suppose,' said Captain James, 'you were to tell me something, Sonny!'

Harris had never struck, in all his two years of Rynox, a similar situation. Harris boggled.

'I . . . I beg your pardon . . .' said Harris.

'I shouldn't,' said Captain James. 'Waste of time, Sonny. Haven't got one . . .' Here Captain James advanced a step further until Harris became acutely aware, not only of the hard stare of Captain James's little eyes, but also of the miasma.

Harris stood his ground. He could not do anything else because he was backed up against the jamb of the swing doors.

'I . . . I . . . I beg your pardon,' said Harris again.

'What I was sayin',' said Captain James, 'was this—I'll say it very slow to match your intelligence! I suppose you couldn't tell me something? That something, Sonny, is: does Mr Benedik happen to be in the office?'

Harris began to get angry. Harris said:

'If I've told you once I've told you a hundred times that Mr Benedik isn't here today.'

Captain James staggered back a step in exaggerated dismay. Captain James stared. 'The little fire-eater!' said Captain James. He took a step forward and then another. Now, actually, his chest was touching Harris. He said:

'I didn't ask what you said. I was asking for the truth. Is or is not Mr Beautiful Benedik in this office at this moment?'

'Don't you,' said Harris in fine defiance, 'talk to me like that!'

'I shall talk,' said Captain James, 'to you, Fanny, just *ex*actly how I please. However, I'll take your word for it that Mr Benedik isn't in the damn'd office. That being so, I think I can dispense with you. Suppose, Bunny, you pop back into your box.'

'I . . . I . . . I . . .' said Harris. 'How . . . how dare you!'

'You make me,' said Captain James, raising an arm of quite abnormal length in proportion to his height, 'vomit.' The fingers at the end of the arm closed, rather in the manner of a steel vice only more painfully, upon the right ear of Harris. It was a large ear and most suitably adapted . . .

Miss Pagan, busy with luncheon-time toilet, was amazed to see in her mirror the entrance, head very much first, of Harris . . .

Harris did not fall. He was saved from this final debasement by the corner of Miss Pagan's table.

Miss Pagan came nearer to showing astonishment than ever before within these walls. She looked suddenly at the door through which Harris had shot. In it was framed the square, thick person and vilely grinning face of Captain James. Upon this face the door closed. Harris was rubbing at his right ear and drawing sobbing breaths of mingled pain and rage.

'What on earth?' said Miss Pagan.

'If I get hold of that blighter,' said Harris, 'I'll . . . I'll . . . I'll . . .' In his right hand he grasped a round, heavy ruler from Miss Pagan's desk. 'I'll show him!' said Harris.

Miss Pagan had recovered composure. 'You'd better hurry,' she said.

Harris threw down the ruler with appalling clatter.

'What's the use?' he said. 'Don't want to get myself the sack.' Miss Pagan smiled.

2

Tony reached Rynox House at four-thirty that afternoon. To him, reading the mail which a day of City visiting had prevented him from seeing before, came Miss Pagan.

'This,' said Miss Pagan, laying down a sheet upon his table, 'is from Mr Woolrich, Mr Benedik.'

Tony looked up. 'I was just going to have a talk with him.'

Miss Pagan shook her head. 'I'm afraid you can't do that, Mr Benedik. Mr Woolrich has gone.'

'Eh?' said Tony sharply. '*Gone?*' He looked at his watch; then shrugged. He picked up the typewritten memorandum and read:

'A man called James (Captain James) called here this afternoon and could not be moved until he had seen me. Unpleasant customer. Would not tell me his business. Insisted on seeing you. I have an idea that you probably will have to see him in the long run and would advise your doing so, therefore, as soon as you can. His address is Croft's Hotel, Strand, WC1. Telephone number: Strand 1234.

'Sorry could not wait but am going into the country

this evening. Will be back, if possible, on Monday. Have
left telephone number with clerk if you want me.

B. WOOLRICH.

'*2nd Oct*., 193—.'

'And who the devil,' said Tony, looking at Miss Pagan, 'may
Captain James be? And what does he want?'

Miss Pagan shook her blonde head. 'I'm afraid I can't answer
either question, Mr Benedik. I can tell you, though, that when
Mr Woolrich writes that Captain James is unpleasant he is, if
anything, understating the case. For one thing, he very roughly
handled one of the clerks.'

'Eh?' said Tony. '*Very roughly handled one of the clerks?*'

'Yes, Mr Benedik.'

'Which one?' said Tony.

Miss Pagan permitted something very much like a smile to
crease the corners of her severely lovely mouth.

'Harris,' she said. 'I don't think he did him any harm beyond
pulling his ear.'

Tony stared at her and saw the instantly repressed beginnings
of the smile and began to smile himself. But the smile as he
pondered turned into a frown.

'If,' he said, 'Harris's ear wants pulling, I think someone in
Rynox ought to do it . . . Yes, I think I'd better see Captain
James. What time have I got tomorrow morning, Miss Pagan?'

Miss Pagan consulted her notebook. 'Unless you have fixed
anything else, Mr Benedik, I think from eleven to eleven-thirty
tomorrow morning is free.'

'Right,' said Tony. 'Ring up that number'—he tapped
Woolrich's note—'and tell this ear-puller that I'll see him at
eleven-fifteen. And I hope,' he said, 'that he'll try and pull mine.
Life, Miss Pagan, is too soft and easy. Ear-pullers welcome!'

'Certainly, Mr Benedik . . .' said Miss Pagan. 'Have you
anything to dictate?'

Tony had, and began it.

3

'Have you ever,' said Captain James, 'seen this one?' He put the red ball half an inch from the centre pocket, the white ball half an inch from the top pocket and Spot half an inch from the mouth of the bottom pocket. All three balls were in a dead straight line. Captain James chalked his cue with care. Captain James straddled his columnar legs and, without seeming to take particular trouble, played Spot. The compact of cue upon ball was hard but the spin was so great that Spot seemed to trickle stickily along the cloth. Just as its collision with red seemed inevitable, it curved outwards past red with a quarter of an inch to spare and rolled lazily on to pot white into the top pocket and follow itself.

'Koo!' said Mr Titchfield. 'That's a one!'

'There's a fellow,' said Mr Bertram, 'down at the Golden Bull does that any time.'

'Ay'm sure Ay don't know,' said Mr Fawcett. 'But Ay think that's just *too* marvellous!'

'BOY!' roared Captain James, slamming his cue back into the rack, 'BOY!'

'You know,' said Mr Bertram into the ear of Mr Titchfield, 'what that means. Doncher?'

'Blessed if I do, except he wants a drink.'

'R!' said Mr Bertram, 'but who's going to pay for it?' He made this remark a little more loudly than he had intended.

Captain James heard the remark. Captain James turned and, playfully, with the flat of his enormous hand, struck Mr Bertram what appeared, at least from the effort behind it, to be a pat upon the fourth of the buttons on Mr Bertram's soup-stained waistcoat.

'I,' said Captain James, 'am going to pay for it! And strangely enough, you lugworm, for yours—if you can drink it.'

It seemed, indeed, very doubtful that Mr Bertram would be

able to drink it. Mr Bertram was sitting upon the worn settee which has stood at the side of Croft's billiard saloon for thirty-five years and looks it. Mr Bertram had one hand clasped to the pit of his stomach and the other to his forehead. Mr Bertram was coughing and gasping.

'Oh, *now*!' said Mr Fawcett. 'Too marvellously brutal!'

Captain James turned his small head so that the small eyes in the large face glared straight at Mr Fawcett. Mr Fawcett quailed in delicious horror.

The door leading from the Saloon Bar swung open; crashed against the wall to make yet deeper the hole which its handle, over the last ten years, had worn in the plaster. Through this sudden aperture came Albert.

'Did edywud call?' said Albert.

'For the love of God,' said Captain James, 'take this'—he held out a shilling—'and go and buy yourself a handkerchief. But before you do that, take an order.'

'Yessir,' said Albert, 'certeddly.'

'Mother Siegel,' said Captain James, clapping the nearly recovered Mr Bertram upon the back with such force that once again he began his coughing, 'what's yours?'

Through his gasps, Mr Bertram got out a word.

'And yours?' Captain James's eyes glanced towards Mr Titchfield.

'Well . . . er . . . Very good of you I'm sure,' said Mr Titchfield. 'I think a nice creamy bass . . .'

Captain James turned now to Mr Fawcett. 'Mary,' said Captain James, 'what about a cup of cocoa?'

'If Ay might,' said Mr Fawcett, 'join you in a crame de mong, it would be *too* marvellous!'

'My God!' said Captain James. 'Albert!'

'Yessir,' said Albert, sniffing.

'One double scotch, one guinness, one bass and a Starboard Light for Gwyneth.'

'Wud large scodje, wud guiddess, wud bass, wud cream de menth . . . Yessir . . .' Once more the door handle crashed into the wall and Albert was gone.

'I am going,' said Captain James, looking round upon his victims, 'to buy you all such a lot of drink that you'll all damn well get tight. I wouldn't, mind you, do this if I could find any *men* to drink with. But as it is, there it is.'

'You must,' said Mr Bertram sourly—he was now leaning rather limply against the corner of the settee—'have come into money.'

The laughter of Captain James set the billiard lamps rocking.

'I have not,' said Captain James, 'but I'm going to.'

Comment the Second

Captain James, so well accustomed to looking after Captain James, seems sure that life is to be easy for him. His certainty has, it appears, come to him after that most inconclusive interview with Mr Basil Woolrich.

SEQUENCE THE THIRD

3rd October 193—   11.30—.

1

CHARLES, who is small and has his torso completely divided by small brass buttons, opened the door of Tony's outer office. Charles piped:

"'E's in the waitin' room, Miss Pygan.'

Miss Pagan turned her blonde, almost too perfect head. 'Thank you, Charles,' said Miss Pagan.

From his table at the other side of the room Harris spoke. 'Who's that?' he said.

Miss Pagan twitched an impatient shoulder. 'Captain James.'

'Him!' said Harris, and then again, 'Him! Oh, is it!' His tone for these five monosyllables told more than the words themselves. It told of what George Ferdinand Harris, Vice-Captain and Treasurer of the Pimlico Road Cyclists' Club would like to do to Captain James if he, George Ferdinand Harris, could only get the chance.

Miss Pagan closed the file upon which she had been working; swung round in her swivel chair; looked at George Ferdinand Harris with that beautiful and utterly impersonal stare which for the first six months of his acquaintance with it had almost reduced George Ferdinand Harris to gibbering idiocy, but to which George Ferdinand Harris was now accustomed.

'Why don't you,' said Miss Pagan, 'just drop in to the waiting room? You might have time . . .'

But Harris once more was busy with ledger and pen and ink. The tips of his ears showed a dark purple, most unbecoming.

Miss Pagan lifted the desk telephone at her side and spoke into it softly . . .

At the other end of that telephone Tony said: 'Have him sent along please.'

'Very well, Mr Benedik.' Miss Pagan hung up the telephone. Miss Pagan pressed a bell, and Charles came running. 'Charles,' said Miss Pagan, 'will you take Captain James, please, along to Mr Benedik at once.'

'Sure will,' piped Charles, who was in the habit of listening to talking pictures. He paused at the door. 'That is,' he said, 'if Mr 'Arris don't want to.' The door opened . . . and shut. Charles was no longer with them.

Miss Pagan laughed; a silvery sound, deliberate, like everything about her. Harris muttered under his breath. Even the lobes of his ears were now that curious dull purple colour.

Charles opened the door of Tony's room. 'Capting James, sir,' said Charles.

Tony had been standing by the window. He came forward as Captain James rolled into the room. He looked hard at Captain James. The small eyes of Captain James met, coolly, the hard grey stare.

Captain James held out a hand. 'Real pleased,' said Captain James, 'to make your acquaintance.'

Tony did not see the hand. Tony said:

'Sit down, will you?'

'I might,' said Captain James, and sat.

The room was silent save for the subdued roar, hushed by height, of the traffic in New Bond Street.

'Well,' said Tony at last.

'Well, well!' said Captain James. 'And that's three holes in the ground . . . See here, Mr Benedik, am I to understand you've seen that partner of yours, what's his name—Woolsack? Tall fellow, about your size, fair hair, bit fratefully Haw-haw?—You seen him since I saw him?' Captain James crossed one short, thick column of a leg over the other. Captain James chewed ruminatively upon that mysterious object which always he seemed to carry in his left cheek. Captain James with his left eye, which seemed smaller and more piglike than its fellow, sent a roving glance over the floor.

'We don't,' said Tony, 'keep them, I'm afraid.'

'Eh?' said Captain James. 'Whassat?'

'Spittoons,' said Tony. 'If you'd like to move your chair nearer to the window, however . . .'

Captain James smiled, showing those irregular fawn-coloured teeth. Not a nice smile. The small eyes glared, balefully almost, up at Tony's.

'Getting fresh?' said Captain James.

Tony shook his head. 'Always am,' he said. 'Same like the daisies.'

'What are we?' said Captain James. 'A cross talk turn?'

Tony shrugged. He walked over from the window and sat, behind the big desk, facing his visitor. Clear grey eyes stared into blood-shot eyes of glazed and faded blue. Neither pair wavered.

'What's this?' said Captain James, 'Hypnotism?' Again the craggy mouth split to show the brown, uneven teeth.

'I understand from my partner,' said Tony, 'that you've got something of great importance to show me. Something that you want money for.'

'Mr Woolsack,' said Captain James, 'seems to have got the right idea.' He put one fur-backed, terrific hand to a pocket; brought it away bearing a soiled and greasy and crumpled envelope. 'Just run your eye,' said Captain James, 'over that.'

Tony stared at this stain upon the virgin whiteness of his blotting-pad; took at last from the envelope several sheets of irregularly folded, flimsy and greyish coloured paper. With this wad in his hand Tony looked at Captain James.

Captain James was smiling, broadly this time. A repulsive spectacle.

'You want me,' said Tony, 'to read this?'

'The folks in this place,' said Captain James, 'certainly do seem to have the brains. That, my boy, is the idea.'

Tony turned his chair so that the light from the window fell comfortably over his shoulder. He unfolded the sheets . . .

There was silence in the room for five minutes; ten; twenty . . . At last Tony laid the papers, now neatly folded, face downwards upon his table. Again he looked at Captain James . . .

'Well?' said Tony. His face was pale; there were lines carven into its leanness which had not been there half an hour before. The pupils of his grey eyes had contracted to black pinheads.

Under the stare Captain James lost his smile and shifted uneasily, uncrossing his legs.

'Do you expect,' said Tony, 'that I shall take any notice of this?'

'I don't,' said Captain James, 'expect. I *know* you will, because you got to! And that, my young cock sparrer, is that!'

Tony did not move. He still looked at Captain James. And Captain James pushed his chair back half an inch. And Captain James seemed to be bracing his body to meet an attack. The eyes of Captain James seemed smaller than ever and extremely wary. Captain James was a person of experience and knew, as soon as any man, when physical trouble was in the air.

'I don't,' repeated Captain James, 'expect anything. I *know* you'll take notice. You can't help yourself, son.'

Tony put out a hand which tapped upon the little pile of papers before him. His eyes never left the eyes of Captain James. He said:

'I know you're foul but I don't think you're a fool. I think I must be correct in assuming that you hold the original of this.'

Captain James laughed, a sound like cracked cans falling down uncarpeted stairs.

'As I said before,' said Captain James, 'the brains in this building must be worth their weight in gold.'

Tony's hand, now clenched into a fist, was withdrawn from the table and hidden below the table with its fellow. Tony's hands were itching, but Tony not only looked like his father, he had his father's intelligence and perhaps more. Tony said:

'And I take it that you want to sell me the original of this letter?'

Once more Captain James laughed. 'Brains going?' he said. 'Why the hell should I *sell* you the original? What I do with the original's my own business. The original,' said Captain James, 'is, if you want to know, Mister Benedik, reposing in the vaults of the National & Shire Bank, Felton Street branch, W1. And there it's going to stay! What I've come here for'— here the face of Captain James was more like the things that peer down from the cornices of Gothic cathedrals than any human face has any right to be—'what I've come here for is just to *borrow* a little "ready." Nothing, of course, to do with anything I've showed you just now. Just as a matter of a trifling loan from one pal to another. It's most unfortunate that mai Bankahs in London should not yet have been advased that I'm a millionah. Until they are advased—and God alone knows when that'll be!—I'm forced, my deah fellah, to borrow. What I should like,' said Captain James, 'and what I'm damn well going to have, is a couple of hundred quid just to go on with.'

'You are going,' said Tony slowly, each word seeming to be forced out of him, 'to have a couple of hundred quid, are you? Just to be going on with?'

He got suddenly to his feet; his chair, thrust back, rocked for a moment; seemed about to fall, then settled itself.

Captain James moved his chair back another half-inch. Captain James looked even more alert than he had before.

'Now!' said Captain James. 'Now, now! . . . What I mean, if you *want* a rough house, have one. But I shouldn't, laddie. I shouldn't! You see, if, before I sent you to the hospital, I was to get some terrible injuries . . . Well, think of my doctah's bills.

That two hundred quid would have to be five, and I should just hate that to happen, old chahp!'

'Has anyone,' said Tony, 'ever told you exactly what a blot you are on the face of the world?'

'Cut that,' said Captain James, and now, though his smile was gone, he was even more unseemly than before, 'right out!'

Tony put out a groping hand behind him, found the arm of his chair, pulled it towards him and sat. He opened a drawer at his right hand.

Captain James shot to his feet as if he had been galvanised. Captain James had seen drawers open before. Captain James' hand went to his left armpit. 'Now *then*!' said Captain James.

'This,' said Tony, 'is not Mexico City.' His hand closed the drawer and came back to the table-top bearing a cheque-book.

'A thousand apologies!' said Captain James. He sat down again.

'I am writing,' said Tony, his pen travelling over the face of a long and important-seeming blue cheque-form, 'a cheque payable to—What's your initial, by the way?'

'Baptismal name,' said Captain James, 'Inigo. To my friends, "Glassy." Owing to my habit of never waiting to draw a cork out of a bottle but just cracking the neck off with my teeth.' Captain James seemed in good humour.

'I am writing,' said Tony again, 'a cheque . . . payable to Inigo James . . . for the sum of . . . one . . . hundred . . . pounds . . .'

'Oh, are you?' said Captain James. 'Are you indeed? I think I said two hundred.'

Tony stopped writing. He looked up. 'You did,' said Tony, 'but I'm writing a cheque for one hundred pounds, and I'm going to ask you, Captain James,—what are you a Captain in, by the way, or of?—I'm going to ask you whether you would come and see me at, let me see, four o'clock tomorrow afternoon, when we could doubtless have a nice cup of China tea together— and discuss some possible permanent arrangement.'

Captain James thought hard. He said at last:

'Nobody can say that Glassy James is hard! My whole trouble in life, son, has been my soft heart. I accept your proposal as made from one gentleman to another . . .'

'That,' said Tony, 'must be very difficult.' He blotted the cheque, ripped it off with a little hishing sound, and threw it across the table. It landed, not upon the table-edge, but upon the floor at Captain James's feet.

'I'm not proud,' said Captain James. 'Not too proud, any road, to pick up a cheque for a hundred. But if you wouldn't mind keeping your hand away from that drawer while I stoop down, I should be *much* obliged.'

Captain James stooped down. He picked up the cheque, but all the time, throughout his stooping, his right hand was below his coat and beneath his left armpit.

'That,' said Captain James, having scrutinised the cheque and put it into a strangely empty seeming wallet, 'is ve-ry nice!' He got to his feet. 'And I'll be here, as you say, to drink a cup of tea with you—beautiful stuff, tea!—at four o'clock tomorrow.'

'Do!' said Tony. 'Do!' His tone had changed. It was now so pleasant as to be almost ingratiating. He even smiled, with an effort which cost him, he explained afterwards to Peter, a stiff neck for three days. But he managed it bravely. He even, as Captain James stood up, thrusting his wallet firmly down into its pocket, extended his hand. He made it of set purpose a hand as limp as a dead cod. Captain James squeezed the hand with his fur-backed five-fingered enormity.

'Ow!' said Tony, by this time well within his part. 'You *are* strong!'

Captain James laughed once more. A hundred tin cans fell down twenty-five uncarpeted steps.

'I'm so weak now,' said Captain James, 'in my old age, that I can't any longer do that trick of splitting a lioness from mouth to tail by getting her upper jaw in my right hand and her lower jaw in my left. I can only do cubs now!'

'I see,' said Tony. His face was anguished. He massaged with gentle left hand the fingers of his right—an admirable piece of acting. He pressed a bell upon his desk, and presently Charles came.

'Charles,' said Mr Anthony X. Benedik, 'will you show Captain James the way to the lift, and will you also tell Miss Pagan that Captain James is coming to see me at four o'clock tomorrow and must be admitted immediately.'

Captain James slapped Charles upon the shoulder. 'Unks!' said Charles, and then, 'Sorry, sir, I'm sure, sir!' He looked at Tony as he spoke.

Tony smiled at him. 'You needn't worry, Charles. Captain James doesn't know his own strength.'

'Goodbah!' said Captain James with another of those smiles. 'We meet again at Philippi!'

2

Sergeant Bellows has been day (and half the night) porter at Croft's Hotel ever since that unfortunate day when, owing to that trifling incident of the petty cash at Halliwells he was dismissed from the Corps of Commissionaires.

Sergeant Bellows' long thin person is so unlike a Sergeant's that his claim to that rank is probably true. He wears, in the morning, a dingy and bastard uniform suggesting almost equally the Captain of a Gravesend-to-Windsor-three-and-sixpenny-Sunday-return-ticket-steamer and a Lance-Corporal in the Bashi-Bazouks. He never somehow succeeds in looking, although indeed it does, as if the uniform belonged to him. He is thin and drooping and disillusioned with weary straw-coloured moustaches and weary gin-glazed eyes. There is, his whole being seems to cry out to you, no hope for Sergeant Bellows; no possibility that ever will Sergeant Bellows do anything but be day (and half the night) porter at Croft's Hotel. Carrying baggage upstairs; carrying baggage downstairs; getting

what tips he can—and these, in Croft's, are not many—cleaning
silver; sweeping, very occasionally, carpets; after lunch carrying
drinks to those residents who want them (because Albert is off
in the afternoons); after dinner, throughout half the night,
dealing (because Miss Figwell, who is 'Receptions,' is off after
dinner) with the steady stream of very dubious husbands and
wives who never have any luggage and who have always done
something like missing the last train back to their imaginary
joint home.

Only once during this year had Sergeant Bellows been seen
to smile and only three times to run, but this morning, Sergeant
Bellows did both.

At two-thirty exactly by Sergeant Bellows' watch a taxi pulled
up outside Croft's and from it came, into the palmed but dusty
'Entrance Lounge' which measured eleven-feet by thirteen, the
cause of Sergeant Bellows' blitheness and activity.

Sergeant Bellows, despite his hopelessness, knew a lady when
he saw one. He also, despite his air of being entirely devoted
to gin, knew beauty when he saw it. And this young lady . . .
this young lady who had come in the taxi and had got out of
the taxi and was now standing in the Lounge talking to Sergeant
Bellows . . . this young lady had both gentility and beauty in
greater measure than Sergeant Bellows could remember having
seen in the past fifteen years.

The young lady smiled at him. The young lady said, after a
glance round the Entrance Lounge which showed to her that
there was no one else within sight, that she wished to see her
brother, the name being Mornington.

Sergeant Bellows put up his right hand in that habitual
gesture with him of head-scratching, but snatched the hand
away admirably before it had reached its goal. He said:

'Mornington, Miss? Mornington? Mornington? Mornington?'

'The name,' said the young lady, 'is Mornington.'

'Oh! Mornington,' said Sergeant Bellows. 'Well, Miss, I'm
very sorry, but I don't recollect . . .'

'Oh, *don't!*' said the young lady. '*Please* don't tell me my brother isn't here!'

'I won't, Miss!' said Sergeant Bellows with fervour. The young lady's anguish had been very real. 'Leastways, Miss,' he said, 'I wouldn't if I could help it. Perhaps the best thing I *could* do, Miss, would be to look at the Register. I don't remember all the names of the people that stays here. Birds of passage, you know, birds of passage. Here today. Gone tomorrow.'

'If you would,' said the young lady smiling such a smile at Sergeant Bellows as to cause that phenomenon of his first running, 'I should be most *terribly* grateful.'

'Certainly, Miss, certainly!' said Sergeant Bellows. 'Anything to oblige, I'm sure.'

He then ran. He ran from just within the doors of the Entrance Lounge to the small and hutch-like office of Miss Figwell. He came out again almost immediately. He was not running now. He was walking and his knees sagged beneath the weight of an enormous leather-bound book.

'Here we are, Miss! Here we are. You can see if your brother's here.'

He put down the Register upon one of the wicker tables which put the Lounge in Entrance. He did this with something of a flourish, marred by the collapse of the table . . .

'Oh, I'm *so* sorry,' said Miss Mornington, 'I'm afraid I'm giving you an *awful* lot of trouble.'

'Miss,' said Sergeant Bellows, now upon his knees and looking up with a queer, craning motion of his long neck which made him look more like an ostrich than ever. 'No trouble at all. A pleasure!'

He rose at last to his feet, the Register securely clasped. He tried with it another table this time and this table was stouter than its fellow. It swayed on its cane legs but remained upright. Together Sergeant Bellows and Miss Mornington peered at the Register . . .

Sergeant Bellows straightened himself; shook his head sadly;

his moustache seemed to droop even more than usual. There
came to his long, thin face a look so intensely lugubrious that
Miss Mornington gazed at him with compassion not altogether
concealing incipient mirth. He shook his head woefully.

'It's no good, Miss. He's not here.'

Any signs of vivacity and the joy of living which might have
been in evidence upon Miss Mornington's face were now obliterated. Miss Mornington seemed, indeed, to Sergeant Bellows'
intense, poignant and yet somehow magically exciting dismay,
to be upon the brink of tears. Her lower lip trembled. Her large,
strange, golden-coloured eyes seemed bright with unshed tears.
Sergeant Bellows could hardly bear it. He stretched out a hand
to pat Miss Mornington tenderly upon the shoulder; snatched
it back only just in time.

'There, Miss, there . . .' said Sergeant Bellows, 'don't you
take on . . .'

'I think,' said the young lady faintly, 'I think . . . if I might sit
down . . . Such a disappointment . . . If I could sit down somewhere . . . No, no, not here . . . Some one might see me . . .'

'Certainly, Miss, certainly,' said Sergeant Bellows in anguish,
'certainly, Miss. Certainly. Certainly. Certainly. This way, Miss!'
And again Sergeant Bellows ran. He ran now from the centre
of the Entrance Lounge to the door marked READING AND
WRITING ROOM. This door he held open.

With a handkerchief pressed to her mouth—a little handker-
chief which bravely endeavoured to conceal her agitation—Miss
Mornington passed through the Entrance Lounge into the
READING AND WRITING ROOM.

This was a chamber some nine feet by six. It seemed,
certainly, that no one could ever read in it; if they had, they
had certainly taken away with them what they were reading.
That someone, however, might at one time or another have
been expected to write there was proved conclusively by the
presence, standing in the window, of a small and dusty and
much battered bureau. Upon this bureau lay a piebald piece of

blotting paper, a crusted ink stand and a partitioned wooden box holding paper and envelopes. Before this bureau stood the room's second chair, the other being a lopsided and horse-hair vomiting edifice which stood before the cold grate in which lay, miserably, a piece of pink crinkled paper whose pinkness was almost entirely obliterated by soot.

Sergeant Bellows, his actions still distinguished by an unusual celerity, pushed forward the mountainous leather chair. Into it Miss Mornington sank with a sigh of relief and closed her eyes. The tiny handkerchief was still pressed to her lips.

'Can I get you anything, Miss?' said Sergeant Bellows, his moustaches agitated by a fervent pity.

'If I might,' said Miss Mornington faintly from behind the handkerchief, 'have a glass of water.'

'*Water*, Miss?' said Sergeant Bellows, incredulously. And then, having collected himself: 'Certainly, Miss. You just sit there and I'll get you a glass of water. Certainly, Miss.' Sergeant Bellows was gone. When he came back, walking as carefully as a tender-footed cat upon hot ploughshares, a thick, chipped tumbler between his dirty, careful hands, Miss Mornington was sitting upon the arm of her chair. She seemed much recovered. She said:

'I'm feeling *so* much better! I can't think what made me so silly!' She took the glass of water from Sergeant Bellows' outstretched hands. 'Thank you *very* much,' she said. 'You *have* been kind.' She sipped at the water and, rising, set the glass down upon the mantelpiece. 'I can't think,' she said again, 'what made me so silly. Except . . . well, you see, my brother is all I have in the world and I haven't seen him for four or five years . . . and . . . and . . .'—a return of Miss Mornington's distress seemed imminent but was bravely mastered—'and I'm afraid . . . well, I'm afraid he's been getting himself into trouble . . . I wish you'd do something for me. Would you?'

'*Would* I?' said Sergeant Bellows with tremendous emphasis, 'you just try me, Miss!'

Miss Mornington tried him. Miss Mornington stammered at first, but, warming to her work, asked Sergeant Bellows whether, should her brother come, under whatever name, he would let her know. Miss Mornington then gave him her telephone number—which she seemed to have some slight difficulty in remembering—and a description of her brother.

'He's tall,' said Miss Mornington, 'a very tall man; rather slim; very broad shoulders; very well-dressed. He would have been,' added Miss Mornington, 'very good-looking if it hadn't been for his accident. I don't think you could *possibly* miss him! His nose is very crooked and one side of his mouth goes up much higher than the other.'

'Just so soon, Miss,' said Sergeant Bellows earnestly, 'as the gentleman comes, I'll ring up.'

'Thank you,' said Miss Mornington, 'you are very, very good.' She rose to her feet. It seemed to Sergeant Bellows that the READING AND WRITING ROOM was suddenly a pleasant place. Miss Mornington, with most unobtrusive fumbling in her bag, produced coins. Miss Mornington said, so charmingly that even a prouder man could not have refused: 'I wonder whether you would be so nice as to drink my health some time.'

'I will that, Miss!' said Sergeant Bellows, taking the money, 'and I might tell you, Miss, that if he comes here I'll look after him.'

Again Miss Mornington smiled. In reply, Sergeant Bellows almost smiled too.

'Good-bye,' said Miss Mornington, 'and thank you very, very much!'

For the last time that afternoon Sergeant Bellows ran. He ran, not only out from READING AND WRITING ROOM, but across the Entrance Lounge and out of the Entrance Lounge into the street, to return very soon, puffing triumphantly, upon the running board of a taxi.

3

'I reelly don't know,' said Mr Butters to his Chief Lad, Richards, 'what's coming over this branch. Why, I can remember the time, Boy, when I'd sixteen lads here and could of done with twenty more. We was that pushed.'

Richards, a youth who would get on, smiled sympathetically. 'You're such a one for work, sir!' he said.

'Well,' said Mr Butters, complacently, 'I do hate being idle. No day is too hard for me. I like to feel I go to bed with something attempted something done. Earned a night's repose. Always have been that way, I suppose.'

The telephone bell at the other end of the counter rang shrilly. Mr Butters leapt for it. Mr Butters whipped the receiver to his ear with a deft click of his stiff-cuffed wrist.

'Yers?' said Mr Butters, interrogatively.

'Is that,' said the telephone, 'the District Messenger Office?' A man's voice, deep and pleasing.

'Yers,' said Mr Butters, 'Destrict Mersengers speakin'.'

'I want,' said the telephone, 'to know whether you can place a messenger at my disposal for the remainder of the day. I have no specific message for him to deliver yet, but I want a boy to come round to my house now'—here the telephone gave a most select address which Mr Butters wrote down upon his little yellow pad with much graceful flourish—'so that he can be at hand if I want to send any messages. I have a very busy afternoon in front of me. I don't know whether you do that kind of thing . . .'

'Cer-tain-ly, sir, cer-tain-ly!' said Mr Butters. 'We're very busy at the moment, of course, but we always do our very, very best to oblige. I think I can get a lad round to you—a trustworthy, intelligent lad—within, shall we say, a quarter of an hour. Would that suit, sir?'

'Admirably,' said the telephone, 'and you will, I suppose, send me an account when you have discovered how long I have kept the boy.'

'The lad, sir,' said Mr Butters, 'will be able to tell you, at the end of his time, what the necessary fee will be. Is that all, sir? ... Thank you, sir ... The lad will be there within fifteen minutes.'

Mr Butters delicately snipped the receiver back on to its hook. Mr Butters turned.

'Richards!' said Mr Butters loudly.

'Sir!' said Richards.

'I want you,' said Mr Butters, tearing the top sheet off his little yellow pad, 'to go to this address at once. You are to 'old—hold yourself at the disposal of this gentleman. He wants your services for running messages this afternoon. Now that's a very very nice little job, Richards; one that may broaden you a lot. You have never had such a job before, I don't think. We don't often get 'em nowadays.'

Richards shook his round, clipped bullet of a head upon which was perched, like some neat but untimely growth, the pill-box hat of the messenger service.

'No, sir,' said Richards, briskly.

'Well, I hope you will find it an interesting afternoon,' said Mr Butters, today in benevolent mood. 'Now slip off and if it's after six when you get away, report in the morning as usual. If you get off before six come back here. Understand?'

'Yes, sir,' said Richard, smartly.

'Right, then,' said Mr Butters, 'Off with you.' He had the manner of a Marèchal Ney hurling four regiments of cuirassiers into action on the right flank.

'Shall I, sir,' said Richards looking at the buff slip, 'take a bus, sir, or walk?'

'Walk,' said Butters, 'walk, walk, walk. I told the gentleman a quarter of an hour and you should be there five minutes early if you use those fat legs of yours. Off with you now.'

So Richards walked. He went on his way whistling. It was a sunny afternoon and he had, the day before, attained the sunny age of sixteen. It may be that on his melodious way he pondered upon what the afternoon held in store for him. If he did, it is quite certain that any answer he may have given himself to this question was wrong. Many things may have been in his mind, but certainly it did not occur to him that he would spend the rest of that day clad only in his underclothes, reading, very comfortably, a wonderful book called *The Coral Island* and eating, for at least an hour of that afternoon, the biggest and most splendid tea for which any boy could wish.

4

Captain James laid down a new and rustling five-pound note with a slap upon the counter. It landed in a little glittering pool of beer.

'Dirty thing!' said Gwen, snatching the note.

Captain James smiled upon her. A smile to which Gwen responded with a challenging toss of the head, which showed that to her at least the odious qualities of this smile were not marked.

'Never mind about dirty thing,' said Captain James, 'you take for that last round out of it and give me the change, ducky. And what about a nice sip of port for yourself?'

Now Gwen smiled upon Captain James in her turn. They had all, Gwen and Mr Titchfield and the elegant Mr Fawcett and three other unnamed customers in this bar of Croft's, been smiling upon Captain James, and smiling steadily, ever since half-past five that afternoon.

'I don't reely mind,' Gwen said, 'if I do . . .' and then, a moment or so later: 'well, cherriliho!'

'Good-night, Nurse!' said Captain James. He drained his own glass and set it down upon the counter with a ringing smack.

'I,' said he, 'am going to knock 'em about a bit. Anyone comin'?'

Without waiting for reply, he swaggered off, rolling his thick, short bulk in the direction of the swing doors leading to the Billiard Room.

And presently, in the Billiard Room, he was playing a hundred up with Mr Titchfield. Mr Fawcett was acting as marker, delicately moving the indicators with the tip of his amber-hilted stick. Two of the unnamed cronies were watching. Every shot played by Captain James was applauded by one of them with loud suckings of his deficient teeth; by the other with a curious snorting chuckle . . . And Albert kept running in and out of the Billiard Room with tray after tray of brimming glasses. Every now and then Captain James would give Albert money . . .

Captain James, with a break of forty-six, ran out.

'Too hot for me!' said Mr Titchfield. 'Lucky I didn't have any money on it.'

'I didn't,' said Captain James, 'have any money on it because I knew I'd beat you and I knew you couldn't pay. Have a drink? BOY!'

Albert came on the heels of the cry, but this time he came without his tray.

'Excuse me, Cabted,' said Albert, 'bud there's a Bessenger Boy. Got a parcel for you, Capted. Says he bust have it sighed for.'

'Well, my Spanish Catarrh,' said Captain James, 'sign for the thing yourself and then give it to me.'

'Please, sir,' said Albert, 'I have tried but the boy says it bust be sighed by you, sir.'

'A lot of nonsense,' said Captain James. 'Send the brat in here. I'll sigh 'im!'

'Certeddly, sir,' said Albert and was gone, reappearing almost immediately followed by a District Messenger who bore beneath his thin right arm a large, square box wrapped in brown paper.

'That,' said Albert, 'is Cabted Jabes.'

Captain James surveyed the messenger.

'Captain James, sir?' said the boy, smartly.

'You know,' said Captain James, 'you'll be wanting my birth certificate next, son. That's me.' The boy set down the parcel upon the edge of the billiard table. It was addressed in bold characters to:

> Captain Inigo James,
> Croft's Hotel,
> Milady Street,
> Strand.

The boy produced from his wallet a large flat receipt book. He opened it and presented it, with a pencil, to Captain James.

'If you wouldn't mind, sir,' he piped, 'signing at the foot here.'

Captain James took the pencil and signed with a heavy-handed flourish.

'And who the hell,' said Captain James, 'is sending me parcels, I can't think.' He turned to Mr Titchfield. 'Here, you've got a knife. Open that, will you . . . Here, Sonny . . .'

The messenger boy, escorted by Albert, who watched his every movement as a young constable his first arrest, went out the richer by a shilling. Captain James, this night, was in a mood most unusually generous . . .

'It's a box,' said Mr Titchfield, through the rustlings of brown paper, 'of cigars.'

Captain James came to his shoulder and peered over it.

'Any message?' he said.

Mr Titchfield conducted an exhaustive search but shook a mournful head. 'None,' he said, 'so far as I can see.'

'*Too* marvellously mysterious!' said Mr Fawcett.

Captain James inspected the square box.

'Floriale Regias,' he read. 'Well, they may be smokeable or they may not.' He turned to Mr Fawcett. 'Here, you shove one of those into your face and tell us what it's like.' He advanced upon Mr Fawcett, determination in every line of him and a cigar between his fingers.

Mr Fawcett backed nervously away. 'Oh, really, ay couldn't!' said Mr Fawcett, 'Ay never smoke anything except cigarettes.'

'You are going,' said Captain James, 'to smoke this Floribloodyale. Oh, yes you are, Mary! Oh, yes you are! . . . Hi! Someone grip him!'

There was subsequently much merriment over Mr Fawcett and the cigar.

COMMENT THE THIRD

WHO is sending Captain James Floriale Regias?

If it comes to that, is it not rather odd that young Mornington was not at Croft's Hotel, especially as he had, it seems, definitely informed his sister that he would be there?

And what about Messenger Richards and *The Coral Island?*

And Woolrich is off to the country again!

SEQUENCE THE FOURTH

October 4th, 193—   9.30 *a.m. to* 9.15 *p.m.*

THE heavy glittering door of the Bank swung slowly inwards. From behind the first *Cashier* notice Carstairs looked out.

'My God!' said Carstairs, and immediately discovered urgent business behind the screen dividing the main office from the counter. This left Wakefield to deal with the customer who had just entered. Wakefield, too late, looked up and saw who it was; cast an anguished glance to his right and to his left; saw that on his right MacPherson was already engaged and that upon his left there was no Carstairs.

Wakefield, cursed with both a perpetual desire to laugh at the world and a cringing horror of injuring the feelings of others, braced himself . . .

Mrs Pardee advanced laboriously upon him. Her ebony stick beat out a slow tattoo upon the marble flags. With her right hand she raised, to mask the glaze of her protuberant blue eyes, a pair of heavily gold-rimmed lorgnettes. Mrs Pardee was very rich. Mrs Pardee was very eccentric. And Mrs Pardee was so mean that she could hardly ever bring herself to write a cheque for more than two pounds. This led to Mrs Pardee's visits to her bank taking place regularly once a day.

'Hoo-hawing!' said Mrs Pardee, who suffered from a cloven palate.

Wakefield, the muscles standing out in great wads on each side of his jaw, bowed. He was making body-racking effort to still the shaking of his stomach which he knew preceded gigantic laughter. He bowed with grave courtesy. He did not trust himself to open his mouth.

Mrs Pardee placed upon the counter a black, foot-square object to describe which the word reticule was obviously coined. In this, after much snapping and clipping of clasps, she dived to produce at length a very small, very thin cheque book. This she laid upon the counter and, with laboured actions, smoothed out until it lay quite flat. Mrs Pardee, reaching for a pen, entered once more into the throes of conversation.

'I wan hoo aw er phmaw hek. Whaw e my baaance?'

A small piece of paper, lobbed truly from behind the partition, struck poor Wakefield at the back of his neck. Having thought that he was now captain of his soul and able to speak without disgracing himself, he suddenly discovered that this was far from the truth. Gallantly he opened his mouth—but there came from it a strange, high-pitched, quivering note . . .

Mrs Pardee looked up interrogatively.

Wakefield shut his mouth with a snap of teeth which could be heard all over the building. From behind the partition there came a sound which was a cross between a cough and a sneeze and an exclamation of agony.

Wakefield, although he knew Mrs Pardee's balance by heart, disappeared at speed in search of it . . . He came back bearing a small piece of paper upon which were pencilled the figures: Bal. curr. A/c. £12,743 11s. 9d.

His face pale, his forehead shining damply, Wakefield courteously slid the slip across the counter. Over it Mrs Pardee bent. After much thought, she began to write painfully upon a cheque-form.

'Hoo-pahs,' said Mrs Pardee, 'chleese.'

This was not the first time upon which Wakefield had spoken with Mrs Pardee. Correctly, he assumed that she wanted two pounds. Encouraged by her imminent departure and satisfied that now he had complete command of himself, he spoke.

'Two notes?' he said. He had meant to speak normally; had thought, up to the very moment the words had left his lips, that his voice was going to issue as a courteous sub-tone. But, instead there had come what sounded, even in his own ears, like a bellow.

Mrs Pardee started and dropped her pen. From behind the screen there came distinctly, to Wakefield's ears, a quavering whisper which said: 'My God!'

Mrs Pardee shook her head. The bugles on her bonnet danced a fantastic jig. Wakefield, in torment, gazed at them fascinated. Now his teeth were biting his bottom lip so hard that a little trickle of blood was appearing at the corner of his mouth.

'I wooh hah-ah hah,' said Mrs Pardee with great rapidity, 'wung pung noh, wung tenh hihing noh en hen hihinghah hur hall hilher.'

From behind the screen that diabolic voice came once more to Wakefield's ears. It wailed now, very low: 'Oh! . . . Oh! . . . Oh! . . .'

With an effort which made to tremble not only the hands with which he laid upon the counter one pound-note, one ten-shilling-note, two half-crowns, one florin and three shilling pieces, but also made his knees feel as if they would at any minute discontinue to support him, Wakefield commanded himself. He was forced to watch while Mrs Pardee not only counted the money four separate times, but placed it, a note at a time and then a coin at a time, into the reticule. He stood, his hands gripping the edge of the counter until the knuckles showed white, motionless save for the ague which every now and then shook him from head to foot. He was now past the stage of coherent thought. The three little wads of blotting-paper which struck him severally upon the right ear, the back of the neck and the left ear, did no more to him than bring on a renewal of the trembling . . .

Mrs Pardee's stick, at last and very long last, tap-tapped its slow way across the marble flags . . .

No sooner had Mrs Pardee's back been presented to his tear-filled eyes than Wakefield staggered along the length of the counter and round behind the screen. He sank upon a stool, put his head in his hands and let himself go. When he raised his head it was to see Carstairs giving a final mopping to his eyes and hurrying back to duty.

'I shall resign,' said Wakefield, tearfully to Tubbs, one of the junior clerks, 'I can't stand it! I *won't* stand it! And if that unprintable blank Carstairs thinks he can get away every time and leave me to look after that far-more-unprintable old woman, he's damn well mistaken.'

Wakefield's annoyance with his colleague, Carstairs, was within two minutes to be re-doubled. For when Wakefield, galvanised by telepathic news of the manager's approach, went back once more to his till, it was to find that Carstairs was talking, more than half his body atop of the mahogany counter, with what Wakefield afterwards described as 'the most utterly, bewilderingly appealing piece *I*'ve ever seen.'

Wakefield stared and Carstairs—lucky devil—talked and laughed and was sympathetic and obliging. Most sympathetic and most obliging. At last Carstairs held in his hand a letter which, with an air of grave importance, he studied. Wakefield noted that apparently Carstairs found difficulty, despite the importance, in keeping his eyes upon the letter; but at length, with a smile and a bow which Wakefield told him afterwards were 'too foully winning,' he disappeared with the letter. Wakefield spent the next four minutes trying to attend to, without looking at or listening to, the wants of an elderly Colonel who wished to pay into an overdrawn account the sum of five pounds and draw out twenty.

Carstairs came back. He handed something—Wakefield, from the corner of his eye, could see reluctance at the termination of so charming a piece of business expressed in every line of Carstairs' beautifully arranged person—across the counter to the vision.

'Thank you,' said the vision, '*so* much.'

'Not,' said Carstairs, smiling fatuously, 'at all. A pleasure!'

While the vision walked doorwards, and for at least thirty seconds after she had passed through the door, neither the small, thin young woman who now awaited Carstairs' administrations, nor the fat elderly one who had replaced with Wakefield the ambitious Colonel, received any attention . . .

2

At the sound of the door opening, Miss Pagan looked up. She saw, pushed round the door at a matter of only some six inches above its handle, the bright face of Charles.

'Mr Benedik,' said Charles, 'told me to tell you, Miss Pygan, that he don't want any tea today. When Capting Jymes arrives, he wants *me* to show him straight along . . . No, don't you fret, Mr 'Arris, he's not going to ask you to deal with him!' Charles shut the door rapidly upon this last shaft of his. You never knew when people might throw things.

Harris, his ears flaring banners of embarrassment, bent over his work, muttering. Miss Pagan smiled.

'I don't know,' said Miss Pagan, 'what's come over that boy today. Seems to be even more sure of his own importance than usual!'

'Brat!' said Harris, savagely. 'If I had *my* way . . .'

'Your way, Mr Harris,' said Miss Pagan, 'is so different always from what you say it's going to be.'

Harris subsided.

'I must say,' said Miss Pagan, who seemed this morning in a mood unusually loquacious, 'that I do wonder at Mr Benedik seeing that awful man again.'

Harris muttered.

'It does seem very odd!' said Miss Pagan. 'All I hope is that he doesn't come in here.'

Harris muttered.

Miss Pagan's hopes were realised. Captain James did not

enter the outer office. Captain James was met just inside the main doors by Charles.

''Afternoon, sir!' said Charles, brightly.

'Good-afternoon, My Lord!' said Captain James, who seemed in a mood most expansive. He smiled upon the world with his unpleasing teeth. His eyes were more notably red-rimmed even than before. The miasma was today an aggressive miasma.

'I want . . .' said Captain James, 'to see Mr Benedik.'

'Yes, sir. Mr Benedik's instructions were to show you stryte along to his room. If you would come this way, sir?' Charles, a small and strutting figure, strode down the carpeted corridor, Captain James rolling in his wake like a tanker towed by a cheeky tug.

Charles halted, behind him Captain James. Charles rapped smartly upon the door.

'Come in!' said Tony's voice.

Charles opened the door. 'Capting Jymes, sir,' he said, and stood aside.

Captain James, preceded always by the miasma, rolled into the room; rolled up to the room's owner with outstretched paw . . .

'All right!' said Captain James a moment later, 'if we want to be haughty and exclusive, haughty and exclusive let's be. It matters, I might tell you, Son, very little to me.'

Captain James still smiled. Unasked, he dropped into the big leather chair which, it seemed to Tony looking at him, he had never left since the interview of yesterday morning.

Captain James crossed his legs and leant the back of his head against the top of the chair and looked up at Tony.

Tony, standing in the middle of the room, his hands clasped behind his back, looked down at Captain James . . .

There was a silence. This silence—combined with Tony's attitude, which somehow was dangerously still, and Tony's hard, cold, steel-grey stare—might well have discommoded ninety-five men out of a hundred.

But Captain James was the ninety-sixth. Without removing his gaze he began to laugh. Not so loudly nor so raucously as yesterday but even more objectionably. Now no tin cans fell clattering down wooden companionways; rather did a toad chuckle while splashing about in a foul-smelling bog.

'Well!' said Captain James, 'come to any decision, Mister?'

Tony moved. Warily the eyes of Captain James followed every action. Tony crossed to the table; twisted his chair with one hand and sat. Tony put his elbows on the table and continued to stare at Captain James. Tony said at last:

'Oh, yes! I thought, you know, Captain, that this was going to be a very serious and difficult matter for me and my firm . . .'

Once more the toad chuckled and shifted its legs. '*Thought?*' said Captain James. 'Ought to say *think*, oughtn't you? Ay mane, may deah fellah, always a fratefully good thing to get one's grammah all rate and all that!'

'I was using,' said Tony, 'the perfect tense, Captain, as that perfectly describes my perfect peace of mind over this whole matter . . .'

Captain James' smile faded from his face. His lips disappeared completely. He uncrossed his legs and sat, quite rigid now, leaning forward. As well as his lips, his eyes seemed to disappear, becoming mere glittering pin points withdrawn under craggy brows.

'The hell you say!' said Captain James. With a movement obviously subconscious, his left hand came up and stroked with soft fingers that something which bulged a little beneath his coat and his left armpit.

'The hell,' said Tony, cheerfully, 'I *do* say!' He took his elbows from the table. He sat back in his chair. He smiled at Captain James. If Rickforth or Woolrich or Rickforth's daughter had come in at that moment and looked at that figure in the chair, they would have thought for a full half minute that they were seeing a ghost. Always had the likeness between Tony and

F. X. been strong. Now, for these minutes, it was something more than likeness. This Benedik said:

'Suppose, before we go any further, you tell me how you came into possession of that letter.'

Captain James pondered, closing red-rimmed lids over the almost invisible eyes. 'I don't see,' said Captain James, 'any harm in that. That letter was given to me by a bloke who used to be in the F. M. S., name of Carruthers—Pinkey Carruthers they used to call him because he could drink more Pink Gins to the square minute than any other man even out there: and that, Sonny,' said Captain James, who seemed to have recovered some of his good humour, 'is *drinking*.'

'Why,' said Tony, not moving, 'did Carruthers give you this letter?'

'Because,' said Captain James, with an evil leer, 'Pinkey Carruthers was cashing in his checks. Fever, plus knife, plus, I've always said, chopped bamboo in his crop. I happened to drop in on Pinkey—he lived so many miles away from anywhere that the fellow must have been mad anyhow—I happened to drop in on him when he was almost on the last lap. He hadn't got anyone he could trust, and I don't wonder, and he gave this to me to deliver.' Here Captain James laughed one of the toad laughs. 'Mind you,' said Captain James, 'he didn't trust me but there wasn't anyone else nigh who could do the job for him . . .'

'The job,' said Tony, still in that flat voice, 'being? . . .'

'Your head,' said Captain James, 'doesn't seem to be as clear as it was yesterday. The job being to deliver this letter to you, or, in the case of your death, to one of the partners of RYNOX.'

'How,' said Tony, 'did this Pinkey Carruthers originally obtain this letter?'

'If you have read the letter,' said Captain James, 'and I know you have, because I bloomin' well sat here and watched you do it, you know. Pinkey Carruthers got this letter by the mail and with the letter there was another letter saying how Pinkey

was to mail this six months from the day he got it. When I ran
across Pinkey and he gave it to me, five of the months had gone
. . . Well, seeing there was something funny about this, I did as
nine hundred and ninety-nine men out of a thousand men of
my acquaintance would do, I opened the letter. When I opened
it I thought to myself "Ah-hah! . . ."'—here Captain James
laughed again and this time not the toad laugh but the cans-
down-the-stairs laugh.

'And there, as you might say, Mister, we are! I've got the
goods. You've got to pay. All merry. All above board. You don't
quarrel with me and I shan't quarrel with you.' Captain James
once more lay back in his chair and once more crossed one leg
over its fellow.

'*You*,' said Tony in a queer voice, 'have the goods . . . Are
you sure of that, Captain?'

'Don't,' said Captain James, 'make me laugh.' More cans
down more stairs and at their end a toad.

'Have I got the goods?' Captain James shook his head in
reproach. 'You ought, by this time, Mister, to know me well
enough to know that when I say I've got the goods, got the
goods I have.'

'I propose,' said Tony, ignoring both the laughter and this
last speech, 'to do this . . .'

Captain James, scenting business at last, uncrossed his legs
and once more leaned forward, each knee supporting a
fur-backed paw.

'I propose,' said Tony, 'to give you a cheque, for services
rendered, for the sum of one hundred and fifty pounds. This
makes, with one hundred I gave you yesterday, two hundred
and fifty pounds, which, for carrying a letter—especially when
you've copied that letter and tried to make black-mailing capital
out of it—is, I think, good pay.'

'Don't,' said Captain James for the second time, 'make me
laugh!' But this time no laugh followed the words. Instead some
more words came. 'Do I understand,' said Captain James, 'that

you think, you poor, fresh-water, soft-roed young skate, that you are going to fob me off with a mere two hundred and fifty quid? Oh, don't, *please* don't make me laugh!'

Once more Tony ignored the remark of his visitor. Instead he put his hand to his breast-pocket. Immediately, with this action, Captain James' right hand shot beneath his coat in the direction of his left armpit.

Tony watched this gesture, and brought from his own pocket a folded envelope. This he laid upon the table so that it and its superscription were easily visible to the eye of Captain James as he lolled in the big chair. It bore, this envelope, the words: Captain Inigo James.

'And inside it,' said Tony, 'is the cheque for one hundred and fifty pounds which I mentioned just now. Are you going to take it, James?'

'Am I going to *what*?' said Captain James. He reached out a hand; engulfed the envelope; rammed it into the now bulging wallet. 'I am going to take it,' said Captain James, and as he said this he looked, though unsmiling, even more repulsive than Tony's worst memory of him. 'But,' said Captain James, 'I am going to take, Sonny, a whole hellova lot more . . .'

Tony interrupted. 'And that,' he said, 'is just where we disagree. You are *not* going to take one penny more. You are going to take nothing more. There is not, if you follow me, any more for you to take, at least in that line.' Tony was smiling now, a fierce, very fixed smile which did not touch his eyes.

'Oh, fresh!' said Captain James, 'very, very fresh! And as green as the bleeding grass! What the hell do you take me for? Somebody's Aunt Susie?'

'I shudder to think,' said Tony, still smiling, 'of your being anybody's Aunt or, for that matter, anybody's relation at all. Any human being's relation that is. I can, however, think of many animals to which you not only bear a resemblance but a blood kinship.'

'Oh, fresh! very fresh!' said Captain James again out of a

lipless mouth. 'Most smooth! But see here, Sonny, smoothness and freshness don't go down with Glassy James. All they do is to make him laugh. I've got your two-fifty. If I don't get more *as* I want it and *when* I want it, or if we don't come to some bigger arrangement, as you might say . . . Well, you know . . . That letter—the original of that letter—gets to places where you don't want it.'

'Oh, *no*!' said Tony, shaking his head. 'Oh, *no*, Captain!'

'What the hell do you mean "Oh no"?' said Captain James.

'Exactly,' said Tony, 'what I say. In no circumstances can the original of that letter be shown by you to anybody.'

Captain James stared. At last, with what was doubtless intended for the parody of a pitying smile, he raised his forefinger and touched his rock-like, mahogany-coloured forehead. He said, speaking as if to himself:

'Daft! That's what it is! Bugs! Flooey! Bats dashing themselves to death against the belfry walls . . .' Captain James broke off. 'What the *hell*!' he said suddenly in a sort of hissing whisper. He stared as if pulled by some invisible force. He got to his feet, thrusting back the deep armchair. He stared, as a snake might stare who suddenly has found a rabbit better at hypnotism than he is himself, at something which Tony held between his fingers, produced like a conjurer's Union Jack, apparently from the thin air . . .

'This,' said Tony, 'is the original letter.' He held the thing up between the thumb and forefinger of each hand, a thick wad of foolscap pages clipped together at the left-hand corner with a rusty brass clip; pages covered with a neat, small-charactered handwriting.

'Look!' said Tony, 'that's it, you know! No mistake! No deception! Nothing, ladies and gentlemen, up my sleeve! . . .'

'How . . . *What the hell?*' said Captain James again.

To Tony's left rear, as he stood behind his table, was the fireplace and in it there crackled a fire of coals and logs.

'Look!' said Tony. Under his fingers the pile of sheets tore, ripped in half across their length, and then, in his hands, the torn sheets were crushed into a ball and the ball was tossed, before Captain James' horrified gaze, unerringly into the fire . . .

A strange sound burst from Captain James. A sound which was cross between foul oaths, and prayer, and the roaring of an injured animal.

The right hand of Captain James came up and disappeared beneath the left lapel of his bulging coat . . .

'Oh, no,' said Tony, 'you don't!' His right hand came up from the table, in it a heavy silver ink-stand . . . The hand jerked . . . There struck Captain James, between and across his eyes, a vicious stream of black liquid.

From Tony's right hand the ink-pot dropped with a clatter, first on the desk top and then on the floor. His left hand came down on the desk and he vaulted. As his feet touched the floor on the desk's other side, his right hand caught the right wrist of Captain James, now, despite the gasping splutters to which its owner was giving vent, grasping a small, stubby, brown automatic. Tony's left hand came up to Captain James' right elbow. There was a sudden flurry of straining bodies; a twist; a wrench . . . The automatic was in Tony's hands.

'Oh, no,' said Tony again, 'you don't!' He tossed the pistol from him, half-turning his body to do so. It slid in a brown arc through the air to smash the glass of a window and fall with a hideous clattering on to the jutting roof of the storey below. Tony stepped back from Captain James. With three movements which seemed like one, Tony took off his coat; threw it too. It lay, a grey, untidy little heap in the corner. He backed away from Captain James until he was at the door; turned, and with one swift movement, locked the door and, plucking out its key, thrust this into his hip pocket. He came away from the door again half-way towards his enemy . . .

'Gord Ormighty!' said Captain James, 'you little blank! You festering little swine!' He had cleared the ink from his eyes with the back of his left hand. His face was a grinning skewbald horror . . .

'If it's a rough-house you're wanting . . .' said Captain James. His voice was not pleasing to hear . . . He stood stock-still, his arms, tremendously long for his height, raised themselves. The broad squat fingers crooked. Suddenly, with a leap almost incredible in its size and quickness, he had abolished the space between himself and his enemy . . .

The door of Miss Pagan's room opened with a crash through which hurtled a small and electrified Charles.

'Here, cummere, quick!' said Charles. 'Here, cummere, quick! Here, cummere, quick!'

'Whatever,' said Miss Pagan, 'is the . . .'

'Here, cummere, quick!'

'What,' said Harris, heavily, 'do you mean, Charles, by . . .'

'Here, cummere, quick! No, not you. You're no damn good. Miss Pygan, it's the Guv'nor. He's scrapping in there with that Jymes. You never 'eard such a row. Here, cummere, quick!'

Miss Pagan, for probably the first time and certainly the last in that office, not only did as she was bidden by Charles, but did it with a celerity quite shattering. Losing, for once, her determined pose of shock-proof calmness, Miss Pagan flew down the passage on small and beautifully shod feet which seemed hardly to touch the carpet. Miss Pagan leant against the wall, having vainly tried the door of the room and found it locked, and put a hand to her heart.

'Oh, my *God*!' said Miss Pagan.

'Didjever,' said Charles, coming up a bad second, ''ear anythink like it in all your life?'

'Quick, quick!' said Miss Pagan, clutching Charles by the shoulder and shaking him in her agitation. 'Quick! Run out and fetch a policeman. *Quickly!* Oh, listen to that! Oh! my God! Go and get the other men and then send someone for a policeman. Hurry, Charles, hurry!'

Charles scratched his head but stayed where he was.

'I'm not so sure, Miss Pygan . . .' he said.

'Oh, hurry, Charles, *hurry*!'

'Now, then,' said Charles, with kindly tolerance, 'you take a holt of yourself, Miss Pygan. This is the Guvnor's job, this is. Now, I know somethink about the Guv'nor and Jymes and I'm not so sure that the Guv'nor'd thank us for interferin'. *Blimey!* Listen to *that*!'

Miss Pagan leant against the wall again, covering her face with her hands. That last crash, a sound as if all the tables in RYNOX House had, of their own accord, suddenly taken it into their heads, simultaneously, to hurl themselves against their respective walls, still rang with its dreadful sound in her ears. And still in her ears were other, smaller sounds. Hissing breaths; grunts—awful, animal-like yet human grunts—gasps; the thudding of feet upon the soft carpet; and other thuddings, reminiscent to Miss Pagan—who had never in her well-ordered life heard fist meeting flesh—of meat and butchers' blocks.

Along the passage, leading a charge of fellow-clerks, came Harris. In each of Harris' hands was a heavy ruler. Harris stopped outside the door. He listened. Behind him his three adherents clustered. They looked at each other with awe-stricken and yet joyous faces. Happenings like this were, alas, far too rare in New Bond Street . . .

Another crash within the room. A crash which was father to all the other crashes. And then—dead, utter silence . . .

'O—Oh!' said Miss Pagan, faintly, and once more covered her face.

Harris, very pale, stepped boldly up to the door and beat upon it with his rulers. 'Here!' said Harris, in a tone which was meant to be deep and manly and official. 'What's all this? What's all this? Are you there, Mr Benedik? Are you there, sir?'

Then, faint sounds within the room. A stirring; then a rattle of the key in the lock; the turning of the key; the door opening . . .

'I am,' said Tony, on the threshold, 'here. But what the *hell* all you people are playing at, *I* don't know! Buzz off back to your work. Go on. *Sharp!*'

Miss Pagan, looking up with joy at the sound of this voice, screamed a little scream, instantly repressed, as her eyes took in the spectacle of the voice's owner. Tony was, in this place and at this time, fit matter for a woman's cries. Not only was he coatless, but waistcoatless. His collar had gone and the most part of the right sleeve of his shirt. This gaped to show his chest, and down the chest were angry scratches, some of them bleeding. His mouth was a mashed blur. His left eye, darkening rapidly, was closed. His nose—the imperious Benedik nose—was ludicrously swollen like a clown's and all over his face were replicas of the scratches upon his chest . . .

'Blimey!' said Charles, in Harris' ear, 'just look at that arm! There's a arm for you! He's O.T., the Guv'nor!'

The shapeless mouth of the figure in the doorway opened again. 'I said buzz off back to your work. All of you except Charles. Come in here, Charles.'

The whole lot buzzed back to their work. *Buzzed* is the right word, for their talk was like the storming of a thousand bumble bees. Charles, swollen with pride, entered the room. The door banged to. Charles looked round the room and a smile of unholy joy brightly illumined his whole face.

'Oh, *Crikey*, sir!' said Charles.

Tony looked round and put up a hand to feel tenderly at his face. 'Yes,' he said, 'bit of a mess, Charles, isn't it? But it was worth it.'

Once more Charles looked around him. 'But I sye, sir, where's . . . where's . . . Oh, *Golly!*'

He had been looking for Captain James and now, quite suddenly, he saw Captain James' feet. They were sticking out from under the overturned mahogany desk. Charles, borne upon the wings of curiosity, took three strides and a jump. He saw—stretched neatly upon his back, breathing heavily to show that he was indeed alive but otherwise with no signs of life—Captain James. He lay very tidily, his legs together, his arms stretched neat and trim by his side. He had, except for his collar, all his clothes on. But his face made Tony's seem what Captain James himself would probably have called 'an oil painting.' At this wreck of Jacobean beauty, Charles gazed with awe.

'Oh, *Golly,* sir,' he said. 'You 'aven't half messed him up proper.' He looked round at his employer with the words. His employer was seated on the window-sill, writing with a pencil on a slip of paper.

'Charles!' said Charles' employer, 'nip round and get all these things as quickly as you damn well like. And while you're at it, get a taxi and tell it to wait.' He jerked a thumb at the peaceful body of Captain James. 'He won't walk home, I know! . . . Here, take the list and pop off.'

Charles took the list. He saw this to be headed by something to do with steak and the last item to have to do with collars and ties.

'Hurry now!' said Tony.

Charles hurried.

Tony, with a heave, righted the desk, sat upon its top and, with much and tender care for his smashed mouth and bleeding lips, lit a cigarette. He sat immediately above the prostrate Captain James and smoked and waited . . .

At last Captain James stirred. Though he might be always half full of Holland's Gin, he was made of hard stuff. Captain James opened an eye, with difficulty owing to its swelling. Tony watched while into this red-rimmed orb intelligence came flooding back.

Captain James sat up. As he moved he let out a grunt like a pig in agony.

Tony stood up. He said, looking down at Captain James: 'Had enough?'

Captain James looked up at him and said, from the orifice which had once borne resemblance to a human mouth: 'By

God, son, I have!' His tone seemed to bear no resentment whatever. Only a dazed wonder. He got slowly and with difficulty to his feet and stood swaying a little upon them. He eyed Tony up and down, the remains of his mouth twisted in painful effort to produce a smile. 'But I marked you, son, I marked you!' said Captain James.

Tony laughed. He felt, as one so often does after a fight, almost friendly towards the man he had been fighting.

'You did!' he said. 'But have a look at yourself in some glass when you pass one, will you?'

'I never,' said Captain James, 'look at myself in a glass, not even when I'm shaving.' He shrugged. He bent his left arm stiffly and searched in his breast pocket. It came away holding the envelope containing the cheque which Tony had given him half an hour before.

'This,' said Captain James anxiously waving the envelope, 'this all right, eh? This O.K.?'

Tony nodded.

Captain James put the envelope back in his pocket. 'Well,' he said with philosophic resignation, 'that's that!' Once more he eyed his conqueror. 'I must say,' he said—there was wonder now in his voice—'I knew they kept smart men in the City of London, but I didn't know they kept bear-cats with brains. Where did you learn to rough-house, Mister?'

Tony shrugged. 'My father sent me all round the world, earning my own way, when I was eighteen.'

'Well,' said Captain James, stiffly and unsteadily trying the action of his legs, 'I'd better be going.'

'You had,' said Tony.

Captain James went, only to come back through the door a moment after it had closed behind him.

'See here,' said Captain James, with something of a return of his earlier manner, 'there's one thing.'

'And what the hell,' said Tony, 'is that?'

'Just this,' said Captain James. 'How in the name of God did you manage to get hold of that letter? If I don't find out, I'll never get any more sleep all my life and you couldn't bear that to happen to Glassey James, now, could you, Mister?'

Tony stood up and threw away his cigarette and went to the corner and picked up his coat. He slipped it on. He stood buttoning it and turning up the collar. He said:

'You practically gave me the letter yourself. You showed me the way to it. Look here! When you were in here yesterday afternoon, you told me that the letter was with your bank. You told me what the bank was and what the branch was and you said: "And don't you forget it!" Well, I didn't. What I did was to talk the matter over with a friend of mine, and what happened then was that this friend of mine went to your hotel and managed to get hold of some of the hotel notepaper. We then got a messenger boy and paid him to lend his uniform to our boy here. You didn't recognise him, did you? That will teach you something, Glassey! That'll teach you to look at boys' faces as well as men's and women's.'

'God Almighty!' said Captain James. 'Do you mean to tell me . . .'

'I do!' said Tony. 'A messenger boy, who was my boy here, went to your hotel last night with a box of cigars. He gave you the box and made you sign for it at the foot of a printed form, and underneath the form was a piece of carbon paper and underneath the piece of carbon paper was a piece of Croft's Hotel notepaper with a typewritten letter from you on it. So that, when you signed the form, you signed a carbon reproduction on the letter. Charles brought the book back to us and with due care we inked in the signature and rubbed out the carbon. The letter was a masterpiece, I think. It was badly typed, but not too badly. It was just the sort of letter that might be typed by a man of your type who used a portable typewriter.

'This morning, my friend took this letter to the bank and had no difficulty in getting your envelope out. The only risk,

Glassey, was that you might have had more than one envelope in the Bank's keeping, but I had to take that risk and it worked all right. I knew once we'd got the original letter we were all right as far as you were concerned. You couldn't kick.'

'May God,' said Captain James, 'strike me a beautiful, blood-stained, ruby pink!'

3

'Your *poor* face, darling!' said Peter.

'You,' said Tony, 'leave my face alone! And I might tell you, Madam, that if you want to see *faces* you'd better have a squint at the face of Captain Glassey James.'

'But was it necessary?' said Peter. 'All the strong-arm stuff, I mean?'

'Well, I had to do *something* about it!' Tony's expostulation came near to the querulous. 'Didn't I now? There was that great stiff thinking he had me on toast and pulling my clerks' ears. Well, after I'd got what I wanted, I had to have the odd word or so with him.' He started to grin in pleasurable retro-spect, but the grin didn't get far. It hurt to grin. 'It *was* a scrap,' he said, 'a good scrap!' He looked across the table of the William Pitt Street dining-room at Peter. 'The sort of scrap,' he said slowly, 'that F. X. himself would have liked.'

'Dear F. X. . . .' said Peter. 'Tony, I want to read that letter again. Now, dear. Got it?'

Tony nodded. From the breast-pocket of his dinner-jacket he pulled the folded sheets of Captain James' copy and handed them across the table. Peter took them and unfolded them and smoothed out their creases with a hand which treated them as tenderly as if they had been sacred things. Across the table— F. X.'s table—she looked at her lover and F. X.'s son. She raised her glass. She did not speak, but Tony raised his too. In silence they drank a toast.

Peter set down her glass and sat back in her chair and once more began to read that letter, which is:

PROLOGUE

MY DEAR ANTHONY,

So far as I can calculate, you will receive this letter about six months after I have been murdered.

I shall have been murdered by half-past ten tomorrow night. This will be, I daresay, distressing for me and I am sure damn painful for you and perhaps one or two other people. My one consolation about you is that I know you will be so busy with RYNOX, owing to my death, that you won't have time to be as put out about it as you would in ordinary circumstances.

Before I go any further, there is one thing I ought to tell you; a thing which, when I have told it to you, will make you a good deal easier in your mind and far more likely to agree with me as to the desirability of my own death. I discovered a little over eighteen months ago—do you remember the time when we were over in Vienna and I had to go to hospital with what I told you was some sort of nervous gastritis?—that I had got cancer. I have seen a good few specialists about it and they all tell me that whatever they do and however much carving and treatment they give me, the thing is bound to kill me in the end. They didn't say as much, but that was what they meant. I am sure you will agree with me that that sort of death is most undesirable. Frankly, from the time I was first *sure* that nothing could be done—that was almost a year ago—I started to think of getting rid of myself in a clean and decent and orderly and untroublesome way. At the beginning, I only thought along the lines of suicide, with an explanation to you. But then—it was in February last when we decided, you remember, to go up to the neck and a bit more over Paramata—I suddenly saw that I could, if I played my cards properly, kill a whole flutter of birds with one stone. Mind you, I knew right from the beginning that to pull off Paramata was not going to be nearly such an easy job as I had told old Sam Rickforth. I'd hinted to you that we were going to have trouble but even to you I didn't say how absolutely certain I was as to the probable extent, in terms of time and money, of that trouble. I knew, for instance, almost to a hundred pounds what we should be pushed for today. And I knew, almost as certainly, that we shouldn't, by ordinary means, be able to get it. And I knew, quite certainly, that if we did get this money and did tide over, then we stood a very, very good chance of knocking 'em all edgeways.

I think you know that you and RYNOX and Peter and a much over-developed sense of humour have been the four big things, almost the four only things, in my life. When, therefore, I found that life was a rotting and shaky and, from my point of view anyhow, a most unpleasing concern, I began to try and find a way by which, in ending it, I could serve the interests of the three other things. I found it like this:

Two years before I discovered there was anything the matter with me, I had, as you know, insured my life—with that colossal endowment policy—for nearly £300,000. (What an awful job I had to get those poor Insurance fish to realise that I was serious over my sevens! If I could I'd have made the damn thing not only £277,777, but I'd have put seven shillings and seven pence on to it. Why, I couldn't tell you. Anyhow, there it is. Seven's always been pretty lucky for me.) I began, almost as soon as I started to plan, to see how this Insurance Policy might fit in with all requirements. I had taken it out with no ulterior motives whatsoever—save the great tax-saving ramp, which is what I did it for—but now I saw how the thing could be more than trebly useful. I saw the time coming, and not far off, when RYNOX would want—would have to have—at least a hundred and ninety thousand, and I saw how, serving all my ends, I could get that money. (It would have been hopeless to attempt to borrow it, even using the Policy. You know that as well as I do. We might have got fifty or sixty thousand, but not more.)

My plan in rough came to this:

To get rid of myself in such a way that the question of suicide could not enter the minds of the Insurance people or anyone else on earth. The full amount of the Insurance would then be paid to you at once and without question.

If I could do this I *knew* that you would immediately put all the money into RYNOX and then proceed to run RYNOX better than it had ever been run before. I knew, in other words, that you'd weather that Paramata business until RYNOX and Paramata were rolling along on top of the world. I knew also that if I left instructions for you—leaving them in such a way that they would not too soon give away my plans—to pay back the Insurance, pay back the Insurance you would. I knew also that if I played my cards properly I could get out of life, in leaving it, one last colossal joke.

I began to scheme. I've schemed, as you know, all my life, but never have I produced a better scheme than this one.

Listen! I am going to be, as I said, murdered tomorrow night. I am going to be murdered by a man named Marsh. That makes you sit up! You've heard of Marsh, haven't you? Sick of the sound of his name! And when I've been murdered by Marsh, the police, try as they will, are going to be completely unable, although they will know that Marsh killed me, to find Marsh. This will annoy them. Marsh is so distinctive a person— not at all the sort of needle one could lose even in the largest haystack.

But they won't find him! They won't find him because at precisely the same moment and by the same means that Francis Xavier Benedik meets his death, so will Boswell Marsh meet his!

In other words Boswell Marsh and Francis Xavier Benedik are one and the same! Marsh, whom everyone, yourself included, will be prepared quite honestly to swear was a man with whom I became acquainted many years ago in South America, actually only came into being six months ago.

You see, Tony, apart from the joke—by the time you get this you will be in condition to see it—it was absolutely essential to

156 RYNOX

make my death not an accident but a murder. Accidents, when large sums are at stake, are always viewed with suspicion by insurance companies; and when an insurance company gets suspicious, God knows what may not be revealed. They are— they have to be—damned clever at that sort of thing. A boating accident; a poisoning accident—any sort of accident was taboo. And so I created Marsh, the man who is going to kill me. It was fun, that creation. My one regret was that I couldn't share the joke with you.

The first thing I did was to buy the ancient diary which is going to prove that Marsh's enmity towards me existed many years ago. Then, a little bit at a time, I began to fake it up. I covered years with that diary, writing up about five years a week. I was full of cunning—most of the stuff was *actual* stuff! I mean, most of it referred to actual and provable incidents. The only real fake in the whole thing was Marsh, and I did him so cleverly that after all this time it would be quite impossible for anyone to say that no man called Marsh was ever in such a place at such a time; that no man called Marsh ever quarrelled with F. X. Benedik. Quite impossible! After the diary I began to teach myself Marsh's handwriting; very soon I had got it not only so that it was utterly different from my own but so that it could be written by me as quickly as my own. And then I set out to *make* Marsh in propria persona.

It took, to make him:

1 black sombrero,
1 walking stick,
1 pair 3/6d. imitation horn-rimmed green glassed spectacles,
15/- worth of moustache and imperial,
1 limp,
1 guttural voice,
2 million Latin R's.
1 dark-and-grey wig (for Little Ockleton use only).

The actual delivery of Marsh was easy. He first saw the light in the lavatory at Piccadilly Circus. F. X. Benedik, that spruce, alert, free-striding and athletic business man, went in. There came out, limping and gutturally cursing, Boswell Marsh. In Boswell Marsh's pocket was, folded up flat, F. X. Benedik's hat; otherwise all the clothes of Boswell Marsh were the clothes of F. X. Benedik. But clothes do not go even a small way towards making the man!

One of the first things that Mr Marsh did, Anthony, was to take a cottage; a little cottage in a village where Mr Marsh's eccentricity and Mr Marsh's unpleasant ways would secure a very full measure of attention from the village gossips. Mr Marsh paid for his cottage, which he was careful to rent from an easygoing farmer, in untraceable notes *at the time of signing the lease*, and Mr Marsh's visits to his country seat (after all, if you're going to make a man, you must show him). will explain all those weekends of mine which, I know, used to make you wonder. From his cottage Mr Marsh, as you will remember, wrote insulting letters to F. X. Benedik. And F. X. Benedik, from his palatial offices, wrote back even more insulting letters to Mr Marsh. Presently the office began (and the office included yourself!) to *know* of Mr Marsh.

Then Mr Marsh began to ring up. I don't suppose—in fact I know they won't—that any one will ever comment upon the fact that Marsh always rang up when F. X. Benedik happened to be out, but of course he did. If it should, however, come to her being questioned on this point, Miss Pagan will swear that there was one occasion upon which Mr Benedik rang up Mr Marsh from the office, because Miss Pagan heard Mr Benedik talking over the telephone to Mr Marsh. I did that today—and got a very great deal of fun out of it—rather macabre fun, doubtless, but fun nevertheless. I left the house in the morning to walk to the office as usual and on the way to the office I rang up twice, using Marsh's voice. I wanted to speak very, very, very urgently to Mr Benedik. Mr Benedik, having delivered, as Marsh, this message, walked on to his office, and once there, not only heard about the telephone calls which Marsh had been making but *appeared* to make one to the telephone number which Marsh had left. How was poor Miss Pagan—who is my witness and a very good one, I should say—to see that while I, F. X. Benedik, appeared to be talking to Boswell Marsh, I had my right forefinger pressed down upon the receiver hook and was therefore talking into an unconnected telephone?

Once—I daren't make it more—Marsh visited the office. I chose a day when I knew both you and Woolrich would be out. You probably heard all about the visit. Marsh was extraordinarily offensive. I can tell you, when I saw Pagan looking at me as I came in I nearly passed away. I had to think very hard of how well my specially built little imperial was stuck on and how satisfyingly well the dark glasses, which were so dark that they would not allow anyone to see anything at all of my eyes, really altered me. I can tell you, Anthony, Mr Marsh's visit, although part of this greatest of all great jokes, almost put the wind up me. Time and again I thought I'd be spotted and time and again somebody—bless 'em!—did or said something that made me realise that I hadn't been. After all, you mustn't forget—as I very nearly forgot at the time—that I had already *planted* Marsh on everyone in the office. I don't think you saw me forcing Marsh down your throat and I don't think the others saw me forcing him down theirs, but force him down I did; so that by the time the actual visit came along they *knew* that Marsh existed.

This seems to be turning out a much more ponderous epistle than I had intended. I just wanted really to explain to you how and why—particularly *how*, as I know your mind works very much like mine. I hope I'm not exceeding all bounds. The best thing I can do to shorten matters is to go straight on to tell you what I am going to do to get murdered by my very much altered ego.

Today, as I have told you, I, F. X. Benedik, have made an appointment (Miss Pagan heard me making it) with Mr Marsh, the appointment being for ten o'clock p.m. tomorrow, Friday, at my house. You will remember that I wasn't at the office this morning. I couldn't be at the office because F. X. Benedik was temporarily non-existent while Mr Boswell Marsh made his presence felt very considerably over quite a large portion of London. You will also remember that I wasn't at home last night, being on one of those mysterious flying visits to what I have always supposed you to think was a 'bird,' but was really to Marsh's cottage at Little Ockleton. The climax-plot began this morning, when Mr Marsh got up.

It worked like this:

Time.	Point.	Remarks.
A. 8.45 a.m.	Mr Marsh receives an unstamped letter from Mr Benedik. Mr Marsh makes a hell of a fuss with postman.	Posted this letter unstamped on purpose to give Marsh a chance to show vindictiveness.
B. 9.0 a.m.	Mr Marsh makes himself unpleasant at Little Ockleton station.	General principles of trail-blazing. No particular point.
C. 11.30 a.m.	Mr Marsh, more unpleasant than ever, buys three stalls at Royal Theatre. Leaves indelible impression on booking clerk.	See below.

D. 11.55 a.m.	Mr Marsh enters District Messenger Office: very unpleasant. Insists on letter addressed to 'Housekeeper and Staff, 4 William Pitt Street' being delivered at a certain time.	Certain time adopted as additional memory provoker.
E. 12.15 p.m.	Mr Marsh, upon the emergency stairs Dover St Station, becomes again F. X. Benedik.	
F. 1.30–3.30 p.m.	F. X. B. lunches with A. X. B. and Peter Rickforth. F. X. B. sends A. X. B. to Paris.	Thus removing A. X. B. from scene of crime and any possible implication in same.

So much for what I have done. Now for what, tomorrow, I'm going to do. I'm going to put this in the same tabular form as today's activities. Like this:

Time.	Point.	Remarks.
A. 9.30 a.m.	I am going to give old Fairburn and the two women permission to go to the theatre. She is sure to ask me.	See how bad this will look for Marsh, who presented, anonymously, the tickets.
B. 10.0 a.m.	Shall leave the house as Benedik and somewhere *en route* become, as I have often done before, Marsh.	

C. 11.0 a.m. | As Marsh shall go and buy at Selsinger's the gun with which I am going to be murdered. | More trail blazing. (Shall probably make it a heavy German automatic, this being the most different thing I can think of from my own revolver which I am also going to use.)

D. 12 noon to 7.30 p.m. | As Benedik, shall carry on in a usual—a very, very usual—way. | Anything to avoid any subsequent suspicion that I knew that anything untoward was to happen.

E. 7.30–8.30 p.m. | F. X. Benedik will dine. The house will be empty except for Prout. After dinner I shall tell Prout that a man called Marsh is coming to see me at ten; that I, in the meantime, am going down to see Rickforth; that if Marsh should come before I return he is to be let in; that once Marsh is in Prout can, as he has been in the habit doing for the last two or three centuries, 'slip round to The Foxhound for a small one.' | See how bad it is looking for Marsh. He has got rid of the female servants and will be assumed to know that between 10 and 11 every night Prout goes out.

F. 8.30 p.m. Shall leave for Rick-   Trail-blazing.
              forth's. Will probably
              take a taxi, but will get
              out of taxi round about
              Knightsbridge   and
              (having changed to
              Marsh   in   some
              convenient place) will
              for a moment or two—
              probably in   some
              pub—behave in a most
              extraordinary manner.

G. 9.0 p.m.   Sam's house and once   Very useful. Sam will
              more in my own appear- make a nice, solid, un-
              ance. Shall talk to Sam shakable, roast-beef-and-
              on business, probably   baked-potatoes witness.
              using the Carruthers-
              Blackstone tangle as a
              pretext. Shan't stay
              very long, but long
              enough to say that I've
              got to get back to settle
              with Marsh.

H. 10.0 p.m. Shall enter 4 Wm. Pitt
              St as Marsh. Shall be (I
              don't think I shall like
              this part much; Prout's
              a good old sort) most
              unpleasant to Prout.
              Prout, you can bet your
              last boot, won't forget
              Marsh in a hurry, but
              Prout, having had
              permission from me, is

| | sure to go out. He doesn't drink much but can't do without that gossip at the Foxhound. |
| I. 10.20 p.m. (or so soon as Prout has thoroughly left.) | Setting stage. This, Anthony, is really damned good. Listen! Marsh is in the house, to everybody's knowledge. Benedik, since shortly he will be found dead there, must have come in at some later time, letting himself in with his key. (Problem: how to kill Benedik, leave certain indications that Marsh has killed him and got away, and eliminate such embarrassing details of Marsh as spectacles, beard and moustache.) I shall (*a*) take the lenses out of the spectacles, put them into a sheet of newspaper, pound the glass into powder and scatter it out of the window, afterwards burning the paper; (*b*) burn until all traces of them are gone—and the smell— |

the moustache and imperial; (*c*) wash my face thoroughly to get traces of spirit gum right off it; (*d*) leave Marsh's most distinctive sombrero prominently in the room; (*e*) get out of the window, cross the path, tie a bit of string on to a tough, long enough shoot of one of the yews on the other side of the path from the house, go back to the study and fix the bit of string so that the shoot is within my reach from the window; (*f*) have a lovely duel between Marsh and Benedik, leaving plenty of signs of it. (I shall stand by the window and blaze away with the mauser as Marsh. I shall then go over to the other side of the room and blaze away with my own gun as Benedik. There will be a nice lot of bullet-holes about telling their own lying story); (*g*) quickly, because people may come in at any moment after the shooting, I shall set the last scene! The setting will prove that Marsh, having started to run away and got through the window, shot Benedik and then escaped across the path, through the shrubbery and out at the other side of the gardens. This will be done like this, ladies and gentlemen—pure deception! I shall go to the window which will be open at the bottom. I shall take the piece of string off the yew shoot, keep hold of the shoot and slip the string into my pocket

Thank the Lord, it hasn't been raining lately and no footprints could be expected to show.

I shall then slip the end of the shoot of yew through the trigger guard of the Mauser. I shall then take my own gun in my right hand and lean my torso out of the window. With my left hand I shall put the Mauser which has, don't forget, the yew

Anyone might have a bit of string in his pocket

shoot through the
trigger guard straining
at it, up close to my
head, but not too close,
and blow out my
brains. What must
happen, because I've
worked it out very care-
fully, is that I shall be
found lying across the
window with my own
gun in my right hand,
shot through the head
with Marsh's gun,
while Marsh's gun will
be found feet—perhaps
yards—away from the
house because the yew
shoot will have pulled
it back and dropped it   Pretty snappy,
somewhere.   what?

And that, Anthony, is the end of Boswell Marsh and F. X. Benedik. Don't—I know you won't—curse me for this. In time you will even see the joke. I'm a rotten life, so I'll make a good death of it. *You* wouldn't like to find that *your* body was going rotten on you, would you? You'd do just the same, but you'd probably make an even better joke of it than I have of this.

Look after yourself, boy, and Peter. And run RYNOX for all you're damn well worth until you're sick of it. When you're sick of it, chuck it, but I don't think you will get sick of it. We've had many good times together and I'm most grateful to you for all of them, and for a lot of other things.

You won't get this letter until long after you've done what I know you'll do, and that is, using the money which you'll make the Insurance wallahs pay you out as quick as you damn well can, to see RYNOX out of the bad times and into the high lights. (I'm prepared to bet you have a tough time with old Sam, who will immediately want to throw himself upon the very doubtful mercies of Carey Street without another word, but I'm equally prepared to bet that you'll stop him from doing it.)

You'll get this letter in about seven months from this minute. I'm posting it tonight to Carey in the F.M.S. (I think you remember old Carey—a very good old friend of mine.) I shall tell him I want it mailed at such-and-such a time to you. He's a stout old fellow and won't let me down, and he's unlikely to die. He's as tough as I used to think I was once. When you get it, perhaps you'll get a shock; perhaps you won't. But anyhow you'll realise that what I've *done* is to borrow £277,777 for RYNOX from the Naval, Military and Cosmopolitan. If RYNOX goes big, pay it back. If RYNOX doesn't go big, you can't and so I should forget it. But if you do repay I should give them 3½%. I leave it to you as to the manner in which you do it. I bet it will be damned funny!

Good-bye, son, and give my love to Peter.

Hoping this will find you as it leaves me at present (very happy),

We remain, Dear Sir,
Your humble and obedient servants,
FRANCIS XAVIER BENEDIK.
BOSWELL MARSH.

THE END

THE WOOD-FOR-THE-TREES

ALTHOUGH *Rynox*—a book which over the years was also published as *The Rynox Mystery*, *The Rynox Murder* and *The Rynox Murder Mystery*—did not feature a detective, author Philip MacDonald was best known for creating the amateur sleuth Colonel Anthony Ruthven Gethryn. Making his debut in *The Rasp* in 1924, Gethryn featured in twelve novels, ten of them between 1928 and 1938, with a twelfth and final appearance in a much later book, widely considered to be MacDonald's crowning glory, *The List of Adrian Messenger*, published in 1959. The Colonel Gethryn books were enormously popular with early Golden Age detective story enthusiasts, with five of them made into feature films.

Philip MacDonald's writing career was not confined to novels, however. He was perhaps best known throughout the 1930s, '40s and '50s as an accomplished screenwriter, and also for his short stories. Twice he won the coveted Edgar Award for best achievement in the short story field, most significantly in 1953 for a US volume of half a dozen stories entitled *Something to Hide*, published in the UK as *Fingers of Fear*. The book was also chosen by Ellery Queen for his prestigious *Queen's Quorum*, a list of the 125 greatest collections of short stories in the history of mystery fiction. One of the six stories, 'The Wood-for-the-Trees', has the distinction of being the only short story by MacDonald to feature Anthony Gethryn, in which the Colonel, returning to England to deliver a secret document to a Personage of Extreme Importance, is challenged by the British weather, a sense of evil, and mass murder . . .

THE EDITOR

IT was in the summer of '36—to be exact upon the fifth of August in that year—that the countryside around the village of Friars' Wick in Downshire, in the southwest of England, was shocked by the discovery of a singularly brutal murder.

The biggest paper in the county, the *Mostyn Courier*, reported the outrage at some length—but since the victim was old, poverty-stricken, female but ill favoured, and with neither friends nor kin, the event passed practically unnoticed by the London Press, even though the killer was uncaught.

Passed unnoticed, that is, until, exactly twenty-four hours later and within a mile or so of its exact locale, the crime was repeated, the victim being another woman who, except in the matter of age, might have been a replica of the first.

This was a time, if you remember, when there was a plethora of news in the world. There was Spain, for instance. There were Mussolini and Ethiopia. There was Herr Hitler. There was Japan. There was Russia. There was dissension at home as well as abroad. There was so much, in fact, that people were stunned by it all and pretending to be bored . . .

Which is doubtless why the editor of Lord Otterill's biggest paper, the *Daily Despatch*, gave full rein to its leading crime reporter and splashed that ingenious scrivener's account of the MANIAC MURDERS IN DOWNSHIRE all across the front page of the first edition of August 8th.

The writer had spread himself. He described the slayings in gory, horrifying prose, omitting only such details as were really unprintable. He drew pathetic (and by no means badly written) word pictures of the two drab women as they had been before they met this sadistic and unpleasing end. And he devoted the last paragraphs of his outpourings to a piece of theorising which gave added thrills to his fascinated readers.

... can it be [he asked under the subheading 'Wake Up, Police!'] *that these two terrible, maniacal, unspeakable crimes—crimes with no motive other than the lust of some depraved and distorted mind—can be but the beginning of a wave of murder such as that which terrorised London in the eighties, when the uncaptured, unknown 'Jack the Ripper' ran his bloodstained gamut of killing?*

You will have noted the date of the *Despatch* article—August 8th. Which was the day after the *Queen Guinivere* sailed from New York for England. Which explains how it came about that Anthony Gethryn, who was a passenger on the great liner, knew nothing whatsoever of the unpleasant occurrences near Friars' Wick. Which is odd, because—although he'd never been there before and had no intention of ever going there again after his simple mission had been fulfilled—it was to Friars' Wick that he must make his way immediately the ship arrived at home.

An odd quirk of fate: one of those peculiar spins of the Wheel.

He didn't want to break his journey to London and home by going to Friars' Wick, or, indeed, any other place. He'd been away—upon a diplomatic task of secrecy, importance, and inescapable tedium—for three months. And he wanted to see his wife and his son, and see them with the least possible delay.

But there it was: he had in his charge a letter which a Personage of Extreme Importance had asked him to deliver into the hands of another (if lesser known) P.O.E.I. The request had been made courteously, and just after the first P.O.E.I. had gone out of his way to do a service for A. R. Gethryn. *Ergo*, A. R. Gethryn must deliver the letter—which, by the way, has nothing in itself to do with this story.

So, upon the afternoon of August the eleventh, Anthony was

driving from the port of Normouth to the hamlet of Friars' Wick and the country house of Sir Adrian LeFane.

He pushed the Voisin along at speed, thankful they'd managed to send it down to Normouth for him. The alternatives would have been a hired car or a train—and on a stifling day like this the thought of either was insupportable.

The ship had docked late, and it was already after six when he reached the outskirts of Mostyn and slowed to a crawl through its narrow streets and came out sweating on the other side. The low grey arch of the sky seemed lower still—and the greyness was becoming tinged with black. The trees which lined the road stood drooping and still, and over everything was a soft and ominous hush through which the sound of passing cars and even the singing of his own tyres seemed muted.

He reduced his speed as he drew near the Bastwick cross-roads. Up to here he had known his way—but now he must traverse unknown territory.

He stopped the car altogether, and peered at a signpost. Its fourth and most easterly arm said, with simple helpfulness, 'FRIARS' WICK—8.'

He followed the pointing arm and found himself boxed in between high and unkempt hedgerows, driving along a narrow lane which twisted up and across the shoulder of a frowning, sparsely wooded hill. There were no cars here; no traffic of any kind; no sign of humanity. The sky had grown more black than grey, and the light had a gloom-laden, coppery quality. The heavy air was difficult to breathe.

The Voisin breasted the hill—and the road shook itself and straightened out as it coasted down, now steep and straight, between wide and barren stretches of heathland.

The village of Friars' Wick, hidden by the foot of another hill, came upon Anthony suddenly, after rounding the first curve in the winding valley.

Although he was going slowly, for the corner had seemed

dangerous, the abrupt emergence of the small township—
materialising, it seemed, out of nothingness—was almost a
physical shock. He slowed still more, and the big black car
rolled silently along the narrow street, between slate-fronted
cottages and occasional little shops.

It was a grey place, sullen and resentful and with something
about it at once strange and familiar; an air which at the same
time fascinated and repelled him; an aura which touched some
sixth sense and set up a strange tingling inside him . . .

He recognised the feeling but wasn't sure if it were genuine;
it might have been induced by a combination of the weather
and his personal irritation at having to come so far out of his
way from London and home.

He reached the end of the main and only street of Friars'
Wick, the point where the small church faces the inn across a
traditional triangle of emerald grass. Here he stopped the car.
He knew he must be within a mile or so of LeFane's house,
and the easiest way to find it was to ask.

He looked around for someone to ask. He saw there was no
human being in sight—and for the first time realised there had
been none at all since he had come around the hill and into
the village.

Something hit the leather of the seat beside him with a small,
smacking sound. A single florin-sized raindrop.

He looked up at the sky. Now it was so close, so lowering,
that it seemed almost to brush the tops of the big elms behind
the white-fronted inn. A spatter of the big drops hit the dust
of the road, each one separated by feet from its fellows. He
realised he was waiting for thunder.

But no thunder came—and no relief. The coppery light was
greener now, and the hush almost palpable.

And then he saw a man. A man who stood beside the
out-buildings of the inn, some twenty yards away.

He was an ordinary-looking man. He fitted his surroundings,
yet seemed to stand out from them in sharp relief. He wore a

shapeless hat, and a shapeless coat, and he had a shotgun under his arm.

Anthony felt an increase of the odd tingling. He looked back along the grey street and still saw no one. He looked at the man again. He looked the other way and saw for the first time the cluster of oaks on the rise away to his left; saw too, above the oaks, the chimneys of a big house.

He drove off. He followed his eyes and set the car up another twisting lane and came presently to imposing wrought-iron gates.

The gates stood open, and he turned the Voisin into them—and at once was in a different world. Outside, the land had been dead and tired and sterile, but here it was lush and well groomed and self-conscious. A hundred feet above, and still half a mile away, he could see the chimneys and the rambling Tudor building beneath them.

There came another flurry of the outsized raindrops, and he thought of stopping and closing the car. He slowed—and as he did so his attention was attracted by something off the road to his right. A figure which stood under one of the trees and looked at him. A large and square and gauntly powerful figure, as motionless as the man in the deserted village had been.

He stared, and for some reason stopped the car. The figure was clad in nondescript clothes, and it was with something of a shock that he realised it was a woman's.

He went on staring—and it turned abruptly and strode off into the shadows of a copse . . .

There were no more raindrops and he drove on, towards the lawns and gardens and the house itself.

When the rain came in earnest, it was a solid sheet of water, a deluge. It started almost as soon as Anthony was in the house—while, in fact, he was being greeted by his hostess, who was blondish and handsome and just verging upon the haggard. She was ultra-smart, and over-nervous. She laughed a great deal, but her eyes never changed. She was, it appeared, Mrs Peter Crecy, and she was also the daughter of Sir Adrian LeFane. She swept Anthony away from the butler and took him to a room which was half library, half salon, and wholly luxurious. She gave him a drink and sprayed him with staccato, half-finished sentences. He gathered that he couldn't see her father just yet—'the man, as usual, doesn't seem to *be* anywhere . . .' He gathered that he was expected to stay the night—'But you *must*—my parent gave the strictest orders . . .'

So he murmured politely and resigned himself, helped no little by the sight of the rain beyond the mullioned windows.

He was given eventually into the care of a black-coated discretion named Phillips, who led him up stairs and along corridors to a sybaritic and most un-Tudorlike suite.

He bathed luxuriously and when he had finished, found his trunk unpacked, his dinner clothes laid out. In shirt sleeves, he walked over to a window and looked out and saw the rain still a heavy, glittering, unbroken veil over the half-dark world. He lit a cigarette, dropped into a chair, stretched out his long legs, and found himself wondering about the village of Friars' Wick and its odd and ominous and indescribable air. But he didn't wonder either long or seriously for, from somewhere below, he heard the booming of a gong.

He put on his coat and slipped LeFane's letter into his breast pocket and made a leisurely way downstairs.

He had expected a dinner which would at the most have a couple of other guests besides himself. He found instead, when he was directed to the drawing room, a collection of eight or ten people.

They were clustered in the middle of the room, and from the centre of the cluster the voice of Mrs Peter Crecy rose and fell like a syncopated fountain.

'Well, that's settled!' it was saying. 'Not a word about it—too frightfully macabre! . . .'

Anthony made unobtrusive entrance, but she saw him

immediately and surged towards him. She was contriving para-
doxically to look handsomer and yet more haggard in a
black-and-gold evening gown. She led him on a tour of introduction. He met, and idly catalogued in his mind, a Lord and
Lady Bracksworth (obvious Master of Fox Hounds—wife knits);
a Mr and Mrs Shelton-Jones (obvious Foreign Office—wife
aspiring Ambassadress); a Professor Martel (possible Physicist,
Middle-European, bearded, egocentric); a Mr and Mrs Geoffrey
Dale (newspaper owner—leader-writing wife)—and then, an
oasis in this desert, his old friend Carol Dunning.

She was sitting in an enormous, high-winged chair and he
hadn't seen her until Mrs Crecy led him toward it.

'And—Miss Dunning,' said Mrs Crecy. 'The novelist, of
course . . . But I believe you know each other—Carol Rushworth
Dunning—'

'Hi, there!' said Miss Dunning refreshingly. A wide and
impish smile creased her impish and ageless and unmistakably
American face.

'What would happen,' asked Miss Dunning, 'if I said, long
time no see?'

'Nothing,' Anthony said. 'I concur. *Too* long.'

He noted with relief that Mrs Crecy had left them. He saw
a servant with a tray of cocktails and got one for Miss Dunning
and another for himself.

'Thanks,' said Miss Dunning. 'Mud in your eye!' She took
half the drink at a gulp and looked up at Anthony. 'If the answer
wasn't so obvious, I'd ask what brought you into this *galère*!'

Anthony said, 'Same to you.' He reflected on the letter in
his pocket. 'And what's obvious? Or has the Diplomatic
Service—'

He broke off, looking across the room at a man who hadn't
merely come into it, but had effected an entrance. A tall, slight,
stoop-shouldered person with a velvet dinner jacket, a mane of
grey hair, and a certain distinction of which he was entirely
aware.

'Enter Right Centre,' Anthony said to Miss Dunning. 'But who? I've lost my programme.'

She looked at him in surprise. 'Curiouser and curiouser,' she said. 'So the man doesn't know his own host. That's him—Sir Adrian LeFane in person. Old World, huh? *Fin-de-siècle.*'

'Well, well,' said Anthony, and stood up as LeFane, having hovered momentarily over the central group with a courtly smile of general greeting, came straight toward him.

'Colonel Gethryn?' He held out a slim white hand, beautifully shaped. 'I trust you'll forgive me for not being here to welcome you. But'—the hand sketched a vague, graceful movement in the air—'I was forced to be elsewhere . . .' The hand came down and offered itself again and Anthony shook it.

'Out, were you?' said Miss Dunning. 'Caught in the rain?'

'Not—ah—noticeably, my dear.' LeFane gave her an avuncular smile. 'I regard myself as fortunate—'

But he never told them why—for at that moment his daughter joined them, words preceding her like fire from a flame thrower. She was worried, it seemed, about someone, or thing, called 'Marya'—you could hear the 'y'—who, or which, should have put in appearance.

She led her parent away—and again Anthony was relieved. He looked at Miss Dunning and said:

'Who is Marya, what is she? Or it, maybe? Or even he?'

'Dax.'

'An impolite sound.' Anthony surveyed her. 'Unless—oh, shades of Angelo! Do you mean the sculptress? The Riondetto group at Geneva? The Icarus at Hendon?'

'Right!' Miss Dunning looked at the door and pointed. 'And here she is . . .'

Striding from the door toward the advancing LeFane was a gaunt giant of a woman. Despite her size—she must have topped six feet—and her extraordinary appearance, she wore a strange, flowing, monk-like garment of some harsh, dark green material. She was impressive rather than ludicrous. Her crag-like face gave no answer to the best of LeFane's smiles, but she permitted herself to be steered toward the group around Mrs Crecy, and in a moment seemed to become its pivot.

'Well?' said Miss Dunning.

'Remarkable,' said Anthony. 'In fact, I remarked her a couple of hours ago. She was under a tree. Looking.'

'Like what?' Miss Dunning wanted to know.

But she wasn't answered. Two more people were entering the room—a well-built, pleasant-faced man of thirty-odd, with a tired look and what used to be called 'professional' appearance; a small, angular, weather-beaten little woman, with no proportions and a face like a happy horse.

Once more Anthony looked at Miss Dunning, and once more she enlightened him.

'Human beings,' said Miss Dunning. 'Refreshing, isn't it? Local doctor and wife. I like 'em.' She looked at her empty glass and handed it to Anthony. 'See what you can do,' she said.

But he had no chance to do it. Mrs Crecy swooped, and he was drawn towards Marya Dax, and presented, and surveyed by strange dark eyes which seemed to be all pupil and were almost on a level with his own.

He murmured some politeness, and was ignored. He turned away and was pounced upon again, and found himself meeting Doctor and Mrs Carmichael. Looking at the woman's freckled, equine face, he was assailed by a flicker of memory.

He shook hands with the husband, but they hadn't said a word to each other when the wife spoke.

'You don't remember me, do you?' She looked up at Anthony with bright, small eyes.

'That's the worst thing you can do to anyone, Min!' her husband chided her affectionately. 'You ought to be ashamed of yourself.'

'If you'll let me have a moment, I'll tell you,' Anthony said— and then, 'It's some time ago—and I remember pigtails? Of course! You're Henry Martin's daughter.'

'There!' Mrs Carmichael caught hold of her husband's arm. 'He did it!'

'And he'd have done it before,' said Carmichael, smiling at her, 'only he couldn't see Little Miss Moneybags as the wife of a country sawbones.' He patted her hand.

'Colonel Gethryn,' said Mrs Carmichael, 'I'm going to trade on old acquaintance. I'm going to ask you a—an indiscreet question. I—'

Her husband moved his broad shoulders uncomfortably. 'Please, Min, go easy,' he said.

'Don't be silly, Jim. You've *got* to try—and Colonel Gethryn won't mind.' She looked up at Anthony like an earnest foal. 'Will you?'

Anthony looked down at the appealing face. 'I shouldn't think so,' he said, and was going to add, 'Try me out,' when dinner was announced and the party began to split into their pairs and he found, with pleasure, that he was to take in Miss Dunning.

The meal, although heavy and of ceremonious splendour, was excellent, and the wines were beyond reproach. So that Anthony found time passing pleasantly enough until, as he chatted with Miss Dunning beside him, he heard his name emerge from what appeared to be a heated argument lower down the table.

'. . . Surely Colonel Gethryn's the one to tell us that!' came the husky voice of Mrs Carmichael. 'After all, he's probably the only person here who knows anything about that sort of thing.'

Anthony, as he was obviously meant to, turned his head. He found many eyes upon him, and said to Mrs Carmichael, 'What sort of thing? Or shouldn't I ask?'

'Crime, of course!' Mrs Carmichael looked as if she were pricking her ears forward. 'Crime in general and, of course, one crime in particular. Or two, I should say.'

Anthony repressed a sigh. He said, hopefully, 'If they're new and British-made, I'm afraid I can't help you. I've been away for months, and only landed this afternoon. I haven't even seen an English paper for a fortnight.'

With a smile alarming in its area and determination, Mrs Crecy cut into the talk. She said:

'How fortunate for you, Mr Gethryn. So abysmally dull they've been! And I think it's a *shame* the way these people are trying to make you talk shop . . .'

She transferred the ferocious smile to little Mrs Carmichael, who shrivelled and muttered something about being 'terribly sorry, Jacqueline,' and tried to start a conversation with Lord Bracksworth about hunting.

But she was cut off in mid-sentence by Marya Dax, who was sitting on Adrian LeFane's right, and therefore obliquely across the table from Anthony. Throughout the meal she had sat like a silent, brooding Norn but now she leaned forward, gripping the edge of the table with enormous, blunt-fingered hands, and, fixing her dark gaze on Anthony, she said, in a harsh contralto:

'Perhaps you have no need to read the papers. Perhaps you can smell where there is evil.'

It was neither question nor statement and Anthony, smiling a smile which might have meant anything, prepared to let it lie.

But the Foreign Office, in the person of Mr Shelton-Jones, saw opportunity for conversation.

'An interesting thought, Miss Dax,' said Mr Shelton-Jones, turning his horn-rimmed gaze upon the Norn. 'Whether or not the trained mind becomes attuned, as it were, to appreciating the *atmosphere*, the *wave length*—perhaps I should call it the *aura*—which might very well emanate from wrongdoing.'

The Norn didn't so much as glance at Mr Shelton-Jones: she kept her dark gaze fixed upon Anthony's face.

But Mr Shelton-Jones was undaunted and now he too looked at Anthony.

'What do you say, Mr Gethryn?' he asked. '*Is* there a criminal aura? Have you ever known of any—ah—"case" in which the investigator was assisted by any such—ah—metaphysical emanation?'

Anthony sighed inwardly; but this was too direct to leave unanswered. He said, 'You mean what the Americans might call a super-hunch? I'm no professional, of course, but I have known of such things.'

The Press joined in now, in the slender shape of Mrs Dale. 'How *fas*-cinating!' she said. 'Could you possibly tell us—'

'Please!' Anthony smiled. 'I was going on to say that the super-hunch—the "emanation"—is utterly untrustworthy. Therefore, it's worse than useless—it's dangerous. It has to be ignored.'

Surprisingly, because he had been silent throughout the meal, it was the bearded physicist Martel who chimed in now. He jutted the beard aggressively in Anthony's direction, and demanded, 'Unt why iss that?' in a tone notably devoid of courtesy.

Anthony surveyed him. 'Because,' he said coolly, 'one can never be sure the impact of the super-hunch is genuine. The feeling might very well be caused by indigestion.'

There were smiles, but not from the Professor, who glared, grunted, and turned back to his plate.

Someone said, 'But seriously, Colonel Gethryn—'

Anthony said, 'I am serious.' The topic couldn't be dropped now, so he might as well deal with it properly. He said:

'I can even give you a recent instance of what I mean . . . I was at the Captain's dinner on the *Guinivere* last night. I drank too much. I didn't get quite enough sleep. And when I landed, the current deluge was brewing. Result, as I drove through Friars' Wick, which I'd never seen before, I had the father and mother of all super-hunches. The countryside—the village itself—the fact that there didn't happen to be anyone about—the black sky—everything combined to produce a definite feeling of'—he shrugged—'well, of evil. Which is patently absurd. And almost certainly, when you think of the Captain's dinner, stomachic in origin.'

He was surprised—very much and most unusually surprised—by the absolute silence which fell on the company as he finished speaking. He looked from face to face and saw on everyone a ruling astonishment. Except in the case of Professor Martel, who scowled sourly and managed at the same time to twist his mouth into a sardonic smile of disbelief.

Someone said, 'That's—*extraordinary*, Colonel Gethryn!'

Martel said, 'You ssay you haff not read the papers. But you haff hear the wireless—perhaps . . .'

Anthony looked at the beard, then at the eyes above it. He said, 'I don't know what that means . . . Just as well, no doubt.'

Marya Dax looked down the table at Martel, examining him with remote eyes. She said, to no one in particular, 'That man should be made quiet!' and there was a moment of raw and uncomfortable tension. Mrs Crecy bit at her lips as if to restrain them from trembling. Adrian LeFane propped an elbow on the table and put a hand up to his face, half hiding it.

Miss Dunning saved the day. She turned to Anthony beside her with semi-comic amazement wrinkling her goblin face. She said, on exactly the right note:

'Remarkable, my dear Holmes!' And then she laughed exactly the right laugh. 'And the odd thing is—you don't know what you've done. Maybe you'd better find out.'

The tension relaxed, and Anthony said, 'I seem to have caused a sensation.' He looked around the table again. 'It could mean there *is* something'—he glanced at the Norn—'evil-smelling in Friars' Wick.'

There was a babble of five or six voices then, all talking at once, and through them, quite clearly, came the husky eagerness of Mrs Carmichael's:

'. . . most wonderful thing I ever heard of! Colonel Gethryn, do you realise you've *proved* what Miss Dax was saying?'

Anthony looked at Mrs Carmichael and smiled. 'That isn't

proof,' he said. 'Might be coincidence. The Captain's dinner was—lavish.'

But Mrs Carmichael wasn't to be deterred. 'You've got to hear,' she said. 'You've *got* to!' She spoke to her husband across the table. 'Jim, tell him all about it.'

A worried look came into Doctor Carmichael's tired, nice-looking face. He cast a glance towards his hostess, but she said nothing, and Mrs Carmichael said, 'Go *on*, Jim!' And Mrs Dale said, 'Please, Doctor!' And he capitulated.

He looked across the table at Anthony. 'I'm deputed for this,' he said, 'because I happen to look after the police work in this part of Downshire. Most of the time the job's a sinecure. But lately—'

He blew out his cheeks in a soundless little whistle and proceeded to tell of the two murders which had so much exercised the Press, particularly the *Despatch*. He was precise and vaguely official. He merely *stated*—but yet, and although it was no news to them, everyone else at the table was absolutely silent. They were, for the most part, watching the face of Anthony Ruthven Gethryn.

Who said, when the statement was over, 'H'mm! Sort of Ripper Redivivus.' His face had offered no signs of any sort to the watchers. It had, as he listened, been as completely blank as a poker player's, with the lids half closed over the green eyes.

Doctor Carmichael said slowly, 'Yes, I suppose so. If there are any more—which I personally am afraid of—although the Chief Constable doesn't agree with me . . .'

'He doesn't?' Anthony's eyes were fully open now. 'Who is he?'

'Major-General Sir Rigby Forsythe.' Acid had crept into the Doctor's tone. 'He "can't see his way" to calling in Scotland Yard. He considers Inspector Fennell and myself "alarmists". He—' Doctor Carmichael cut himself off abruptly.

But Anthony finished the sentence for him, '—refuses to

realise that two brutal murders, apparently carried out by a sexual maniac, could possibly be the beginning of a series. That it?'

'Precisely!' Doctor Carmichael brightened at this ready understanding. 'And he goes on refusing to realise, in spite of the fact that Fennel's tried a hundred times to show him that as the death of either of those poor women couldn't conceivably have benefited anyone, the murders must have been done by a maniac.' A faint expression of disgust passed over Doctor Carmichael's face. 'A peculiarly revolting maniac! And maniacs who've found a way of gratifying their mania—well, they don't stop . . .'

'For mysself,' came the harshly sibiliant voice of Professor Martel, 'I do not think a maniac.' He was sitting back in his chair now, the beard tilted upward. 'I think a public benefactor.'

He paused and there came the slightly bewildered silence he had obviously expected. He said:

'Thosse women! Thosse creaturess! I haff sseen them both while they were alife. They sserved no purpose and they were hideouss! The worlt is better less them.'

Now the silence was shocked. It was broken by Marya Dax. Again she looked down the table toward Martel, and again seemed to examine him. She said:

'There is one hideous thing here with us. It is your mind.' She ceased to examine the man, and went on:

'No human body,' she said, 'is completely without beauty.'

'Oh, come now, my dear Miss Dax,' said Lady Bracksworth surprisingly, in a mild but determined little voice. 'Although I have nothing but sympathy'—she darted a look of dislike toward Martel—'for those poor unfortunate women, I must say that at least one of them—Sarah Paddock, I mean—was a truly disgraceful object.'

The Norn turned slow and blazing eyes upon this impudence.

'This woman,' said the Norn, 'this Paddock—I suppose you

did not ever look at her hands?' She said, 'They were dirty always. They were harsh with work. But they were beautiful.'

'An interesting thought indeed!' said Mr Shelton-Jones. 'Can beauty in the—ah—human frame be considered, as it were, in *units*—or must it be, before we recognise it, a totality of such units?'

Mrs Carmichael said, 'I think Miss Dax is right.' She looked over at her husband. 'Don't you think so?'

He smiled at her, but didn't answer and she said insistently, 'Isn't she right, Jim? You think she is, don't you?'

'Of course she is,' Carmichael said. He looked around the table. 'In my profession I see a great many human bodies. And I see a great many'—he looked at Mr Shelton-Jones—'beautiful "units" in otherwise ugly specimens. For instance'—he looked at Marya Dax—'I particularly noticed poor Sarah Paddock's hands.'

Mr Shelton-Jones settled his spectacles more firmly astride his nose. 'But, my dear sir—if I may be permitted to support my original contention—what beauty can there be in a "beauty unit" if such unit is mere island, as it were, in an ocean of ugliness?' Obviously prepared for debate, he leaned back in his chair, fixing his gaze upon Doctor Carmichael.

Carmichael said, 'Plenty. You can't deny, for instance, that Sarah Paddock's hands were beautiful in themselves.' He seemed nettled by the parliamentary manner of Mr Shelton-Jones. 'Suppose Miss Dax had modelled them!'

'Then,' Mr Shelton-Jones blandly observed, 'they would have been apart from their hideous surroundings.'

'Euclidian,' said Anthony. 'Some of the parts may or may not be equal to their total.'

But Doctor Carmichael went on looking at Mr Shelton-Jones.

'All right,' said Doctor Carmichael. 'Suppose you saw magnificent shoulders on a—on an extreme case of *lupus vulgaris*. Would the horrible condition of the face and neck make the shoulders repulsive too?'

'The whole picture would be—ah—definitely unpleasing.' Mr Shelton-Jones was blandness itself and the Norn turned her dark, examining gaze upon him.

Colour had risen to Doctor Carmichael's face. He stared hard at Mr Shelton-Jones and said:

'Let's try again. Do you mean to tell me that if you saw titian hair on a typical troglodytic head, you'd think it was ugly, because of its setting?'

'I agree with the Doctor,' said the Norn. 'The other killed woman—her name I forget—was worse formed than the first. But the shape of her skull was noble.'

'Umpf-chnff!' remarked Lord Bracksworth. 'That'd be the fortune-tellin' one, the Stebbins woman . . . D'ja know, I was talkin' to that Inspector fellah s'mornin', and he was tellin' me that when they found her, this old gal—'

At the head of the table, Adrian LeFane sat suddenly upright. He brought his open hand violently down upon the cloth, so that the glasses beside his plate chimed and jingled.

'*Please!*' His face twisted as if with physical pain. 'Let us have no more of this—this—intolerable *ugliness!*'

It was about an hour after dinner—which, thanks mainly to the social genius of Miss Dunning, had ended on a subdued but unembarrassing note—that Mrs Carmichael, her husband in attendance, contrived to corner Anthony in a remote quarter of the vast drawing room.

He had just come in after a visit to Adrian LeFane's study, where he had at last delivered the letter which has nothing to do with this tale. He allowed himself to be cornered, although he would much rather have talked with Miss Dunning, because there was something desperately appealing in the filly-like gaze of Mrs Carmichael.

She said, 'Oh, please, Colonel Gethryn, *may* we talk to you?' Her long, freckled face was as earnest as her voice.

Anthony said, 'Why not?'

Carmichael said, 'Oh, Min, why insist on worrying the man?' He gave Anthony a little apologetic smile.

'Because it's worrying *you*, darling!' Mrs Carmichael laid a hand on her husband's arm, but went on looking at Colonel Gethryn.

'Jim's terribly upset,' she said, 'about that horrid old Chief Constable. He thinks—I mean, Jim does—that the Downshire police can't possibly catch this dreadful murderer unless they get help from Scotland Yard. And they can't get it unless the Chief Constable asks for it—'

Her husband interrupted. 'For heaven's sake, dear, Gethryn knows all about that sort of thing!'

She paid no attention to him. She said to Anthony, 'And what I was going to ask you: we wondered if there was any way—any way at all—you could use your influence to—'

She left the sentence in mid-air as she caught sight of a servant approaching her husband.

'Doctor Carmichael,' said the man. He lowered his voice, but his words came clearly. 'Excuse me, sir, but there's an important message for you.' A curious blend of horrified dismay and cassandrine pleasure showed through his servitor's mask. He said:

'Inspector Fennel telephoned. There's been another of these dreadful murders. He wants you to come at once, sir, to Pilligrew Lane, where it comes out by Masham's . . .'

'Just around the next corner,' said Doctor Carmichael, and braked hard.

Beside him, Anthony grunted—he never has liked and never will like being driven.

The little car skidded around a sharp turn and into the mouth of a lane which lay dark and narrow between a high hedge and the looming backs of three great barns.

Through the steady glittering sheet of the rain, a group of men and cars showed ahead, barring the way completely and standing out black in the concentrated glare of headlights.

Carmichael stopped his engine and scrambled out. Anthony followed and felt the sweeping of the rain down over him and the seeping of viscous mud through his thin shoes. He followed Carmichael toward the group and a figure turned from it, advancing on them and flashing an electric torch—a man in a heavy black stormcoat and the flat, visored cap of a uniformed Police Inspector.

Carmichael said, 'Fennel, this is Colonel Gethryn—' and didn't get any farther because the man, having darted a look at Anthony, turned back to him in amazement.

'But, Doctor,' said Inspector Fennell, in a hoarse and confidential whisper, 'Sir Rigby's done it already. Did it last night, without saying a word to me. Called London and got the Commissioner, and turned up, after I'd phoned him about this, all complete with a Detective-Inspector just arrived from the Yard!'

Carmichael stared as if he couldn't believe his ears, and Anthony said to Fennel, 'Who did they send? Hobday?'

Fennel said, 'That's right, sir,' and led the way toward the group in the light.

They slithered after him through the mud, and in a moment Hobday was looking at Anthony and saying, 'Good Lord, sir, where did *you* drop from?'

And then there was a word with Sir Rigby Forsythe, who seemed somewhat taken aback by Anthony's presence, and a moment or so of waiting while the photographers finished their work over what lay in the ditch against the hedge.

Anthony said, 'This new victim? I suppose it's a woman—but what kind? Was she another local character?'

Fennel said, 'Yes, she's a woman all right, sir. And it's—it's horrible, worse than the others.' He glanced toward the ditch and quickly away again. He seemed to realise he had strayed most unprofessionally from the point, and cleared his throat. 'I don't think she's—she was a local, sir. So far nobody's recognised her. Seems to've been one of those gypsy basket menders.

She had an old horse and cart—prob'ly was just passing through on her way to Deyning.'

Hobday said, 'If it hadn't been for the horse, we wouldn't have known yet. But a farm labourer found it wandering and began to look for its owner.'

The photographers finished their work, and one of them came up to the Chief Constable and saluted. 'All through, sir,' he said, his voice shaky and uncertain.

Sir Rigby Forsythe looked at Anthony, then at Carmichael and the others. His weather-beaten face was lined and pallid. He said, 'You fellahs go ahead. I've seen all I need.' He stood where he was while Fennell, visibly conquering reluctance, led the way with Carmichael, and Hobday and Anthony followed.

The headlights of the police cars cut through the water-drenched darkness. They made a nightmare tableau of the thing which lay half in and half out of the ditch. Anthony muttered, 'God!' and the usually stolid Hobday drew in his breath with a little hiss. Carmichael, his face set and grim, dropped on his knees in the oozing mud. He made a cursory examination.

Then he stood up. 'All right,' he said. 'We can move her now,' and then, helped by Anthony and Hobday, lifted the thing and set it upon clean wet grass and in merciful shadow. He straightened the saturated rags of its clothing, and then suddenly dropped on one knee again and said, 'Anyone got a torch?'

Hobday gave him one, and he shone the light on the head and gently moved the heavy mud-covered mass of red hair away from the features it was covering.

'Just wondering whether I'd ever seen her' he said. He kept the light of the torch on the face and it stared up at them, washed cleaner every moment by the flooding rain. It was a brutish, sub-human face, and although it was distorted by death and terror, it could have been little more prepossessing in life.

Carmichael shook his head. 'No,' he said. 'They're right. She's a stranger round here.' He switched off the torch, but

Anthony said, 'Just a minute,' and took it from him and knelt beside the body himself and switched the light on again and peered at the throat, where a darkness like a big bruise showed in the hollow below the chin.

But after a moment, he too shook his head. 'No. It's a birth-mark,' he said, and Carmichael peered at it and said, 'Yes. Or possibly an old scar.'

They stood up, and Hobday took the torch and knelt in his turn and began a slow, methodical examination of the clothing.

Anthony said, 'Silly question, I know, but about how long since death?' A little cascade of water tumbled from his hatbrim as he bent his head to button his raincoat, which had come undone.

Carmichael said, 'Oh—very loosely, and subject to error—not more than five hours, not less than two.'

Anthony looked at his watch, whose glowing figures said eleven forty-five, and found himself calculating times. But this didn't get him anywhere, and he was glad when, thirty minutes later, he found himself being driven back to LeFane's house by Carmichael. He said to Carmichael on the way:

'You see, it's definitely not my sort of thing. Mass murders are mad murders, and mad murders, in the ordinary sense of the word, are motiveless. Which makes them a matter for routine policio-military methods. At which I'm worse than useless, while men like Hobday are solid and brilliant at the same time.'

Carmichael smiled. 'I'm glad you're both here—Hobday and yourself. I'll sleep better tonight than I have for a week.'

They reached the house and were no sooner in the big hall than they were surrounded. They were plied with drinks and food, and besieged with questions. Was it really another of the *same* murders? Where had it happened? Was the victim the same *sort* of person? Did they think the murderer would be caught this time? Wasn't there something terribly *wrong* with police methods when things like this were allowed to go on? Wouldn't it be a good idea to have a curfew, or a registration every day of the movements of every man, woman and child in the district?

Mr Shelton-Jones said, 'An interesting point. How far may the liberties of the individual be restricted when such restriction is—ah—for the purpose of protecting the community?'

Miss Dunning said, 'Human beings are terrifying, aren't they?'

Professor Martel said, 'I woult like to know—wass thiss one usseless and hideouss like the otherss?'

Mrs Carmichael said, 'Oh, *had* Sir Rigby sent for Scotland Yard *already*? Oh, thank *goodness*!'

Everyone said something. Except Adrian LeFane and Marya Dax. And they were not present.

Anthony, throwing aside civility, at last forced his way upstairs. It seemed to him that he was even more grateful than the Carmichaels for the advent of Detective-Inspector Hobday.

He made ready for bed and then, smoking a last cigarette and wondering how soon in the morning he could decently leave, strolled over to a window.

The rain had stopped now and a pale moon shone through clouds on to the sodden earth. By the watery light he saw a figure striding up the steps of a terrace beneath him, making for the house. It was tall and powerful and square-shouldered and unmistakable in spite of its shapeless coat and headgear.

He watched it until it was out of sight beneath him. He heard a door open and close.

He went over to the bed and sat on the edge of it and finished the cigarette. He pondered. He stubbed out the cigarette at last and got into bed. After all, if sculptresses liked to walk at night, why shouldn't they?

But he knew he would stop on his way home tomorrow and have a word with Hobday.

He went to sleep.

*

It was six o'clock on the next afternoon. He had been in London and at home since one. He sat in the library at Stukely Gardens with his wife and his son.

A violent storm had replaced yesterday's deluge. It had raged intermittently over London and the whole south of England since early morning, and still the hard, heavy rain drove against the windows, while thunder rumbled and great flashes of lightning kept tearing the half darkness.

Master Alan Gethryn gave his approval to the weather. 'It sort of makes it all small and comf'table in here,' he said, looking up from the jigsaw puzzle strewn about the floor.

Anthony said, 'I know exactly what you mean,' and looked at his wife, who sat on the arm of his chair.

Master Alan Gethryn pored over the puzzle—an intricate forest scene of which he had only one corner done. He sighed and scratched his head, and then suddenly laughed.

'It's like what Mr Haslam's always saying,' he said—and Lucia looked at Anthony and explained *sotto voce*, 'Master at the new school,' and then said to her son, 'What d'you mean, old boy?'

He looked up at her, still smiling. 'He's *always* saying, "You chaps can't see the wood for the trees."' He chuckled. 'Like this puzzle.'

Sublimely unconscious of the effect his words had had upon his father, he returned to his labours.

But Lucia, watching her husband's face, was concerned. She had to wait until her son had left them and gone supperwards, but the moment the door had closed behind him, she stood over Anthony and looked down at him and said:

'What's the matter, darling? You've got that look. What did Alan say?'

Anthony reached up a long arm and pulled her down on to his knees. 'He gave me an idea—unintentionally, of course.' He kissed her. 'A damned nasty, uncomfortable idea. I'd like to forget about it.'

Lucia said, 'You know you won't. So you'd better tell me.'

Anthony said, 'Suppose I wanted to kill someone—let's say, your Uncle Perceval. And suppose his demise would benefit me to such an extent that I was afraid a nice straight murder would inevitably point at me. And suppose I were that most dangerous of madmen, the secret megalomaniac, and utterly ruthless to boot. So suppose I started a wave of apparently insane slayings, and got well going with three murders of middle-aged clubmen I didn't know at all—and then killed Uncle Perceval in exactly the same way—and then killed three more middle-aged clubmen! The police would be chasing a madman with an extraordinary quirk. They wouldn't dream of chasing me!'

'What loathsome thoughts you do have!' Lucia turned her head to look at his face. 'Oh, Anthony—is that just an idea? Or do you think it's what's happenind in Downshire?'

'Oh, just an idea,' said Anthony slowly. 'It doesn't fit . . .'

She dropped a kiss on his forehead and stood up. She said, 'I'll get you a drink. And after that, my lad, you've got to change—we're due at the Dufresnes's by eight. White tie.'

She started to cross the room, then checked. She said:

'What on earth did Alan say that gave you that dreadful notion?'

Anthony looked at her. 'My dear girl!' he said. '"You can't see the wood for the trees" . . .'

Lucia shivered, went out of the room, came back with his drink, and very soon herded him upstairs.

Forty-five minutes later she walked into his dressing room. He was tying his tie, and he saw her in the mirror and said, 'You know, Americans really develop the possibilities of our language. Baby, you look like a million dollars!'

She said, 'I love you. But we're going to be late and then I won't.'

He put the finishing touches to the bow. 'Get my coat, beldame,' he said, and started to distribute keys and money and cigarette case among his pockets.

Lucia crossed toward the big wardrobe. Beside it was Anthony's trunk, and on a nearby chair a neat pile of the clothing with which he had travelled. Something about the pile caught Lucia's eye, and she stopped and looked down at it. She said:

'Whatever happened to this dinner jacket?'

'Rain last night,' Anthony said. 'White'll see to it.'

She smiled. Carefully she picked something from the shoulder of the black coat. She said, 'He ought to've seen to this, oughtn't he? Before *I* saw it!'

She went toward him, carrying her hands in front of her, one above the other and a good two feet apart.

'Magnificent!' said Anthony. 'Most impressive! But what's the role?'

She came close to him. She moved her hands and there was a glint of light from the apparent emptiness between them.

He saw a long hair of glittering reddish-gold.

He said, 'Not Guilty, M'lud,' and looked at the hair again.

He said, 'Nobody at LeFane's had that colour. Or length . . .'

He said, 'Good *God*!'

He jumped across the room and snatched at the telephone.

And two minutes later was being informed that, owing to storm damage, all the trunk lines to Downshire were out of order . . .

He began to tear off the dress clothes. He said, 'Get them to bring round the car! Quick!'

Little Mrs Carmichael lay on the rather uncomfortable couch in the living room of Doctor Carmichael's rather uncomfortable house. She was pretending to read but really she was listening to the thunder.

She wished Jim hadn't had to go out on a call, especially on a night like this. She thought about Jim and how wonderful he was. Although it was two years now since they'd been married, she was happier than she had been on her honeymoon.

Happy—and proud. Proud of Jim, and proud of herself, too; proud that she didn't mind uncomfortable sofas and cups with chips in them and a gas fire in the bedroom. Proud of her cleverness—her really heaven-inspired cleverness—in realizing right at the start, even before they were married, that a man of Jim's calibre couldn't possibly bear living on his wife's money . . .

The thunder was far away now, and almost casual. Little Mrs Carmichael dozed . . .

She was wakened by the sound of a key in the front door—Jim's key. She heard Jim's step in the hall and jumped up off the sofa and went to the door to meet him—and then was shocked by his appearance as he threw it open just before she reached it. He had his hat on still, and his raincoat. They were both dark and dripping with water. He was frowning, and his face was very white; there was a look in his eyes she'd never seen before.

She said, 'Jim! What is it, dearest? What's *happened*?'

'Accident,' he said. 'I ran over someone . . .' He pulled the back of a hand across his forehead so that his hat was pushed back and she noticed, with utter irrelevance, the little red line which the brim had made across the skin.

He said, 'Come and help me, will you? Put on a coat and run out to the car. He's in the back seat.' He turned away and strode across the hall to the surgery door. 'With you in a minute,' he said.

She ran to the hall cupboard and dragged out a raincoat. She tugged open the front door and hurried down the path, the uneven brick slippery under her feet.

The gate was open and through the rain she could see the dark shape of Jim's car. She stumbled toward it and pulled open the door and the little light in the roof came on.

There was nothing in the back seat.

Bewildered, she turned—and there was Jim, close to her.

She started to say something—and then she saw Jim's face—

It *was* Jim's face—but she almost didn't recognize it. And

there was something bright in his hand, something bright and sharp and terrifying.

She screamed—and suddenly everything went very fast in front of her eyes, the way things used to go fast in films when she was a child, and there was a shouting of men's voices, and something heavy like a stone swished through the air past her and hit Jim on the head, and he fell down and the bright steel thing dropped out of his hand, and two men ran up, and one of them was Colonel Gethryn and the other knelt over Jim, and Colonel Gethryn put his arm around her as she swayed on her feet, and the black wet world spun dizzily . . .

'But there isn't anything complex about it,' said Anthony. 'I started when my son gave me the "can't-see-the-wood-for-the-trees" idea. And then Lucia found that long, magnificent, red-gold hair on my dinner jacket. And that's all there was to it . . .'

The others said a lot of things, together and separately.

He waited for them to finish, and then shook his head sadly.

He said, 'My dear people, that hair was tantamount to a confession by Doctor James Carmichael, duly signed, attested and registered at Somerset House. I might never have realised it, of course, if Alan hadn't handed me "wood-for-the-trees." But as I'd evolved the notion of hiding one murder with a lot of other murders—well, it was completely obvious. Carmichael, whose wife was rich and plain and overloving, fitted everything. He was a doctor. He could travel about. He—'

'But *why* did the hair necessarily point to him?'

'Because it must have come from the third body. Because no one at LeFane's had hair even remotely red. Of course, it was caked with mud and colourless when it got on to my coat, but by the time it dried—'

'Hold it! Hold it! I *still* don't see how it pointed to the doctor!'

'I'm surprised at you!' Anthony surveyed the speaker with real astonishment.

'After all, you were there at LeFane's. You heard Carmichael arguing with that horn-rimmed intellect from the Foreign Office. Don't you remember him talking about *titian hair on troglodytes*?'

'Why, yes . . . But—'

'Don't you realize he talked *too soon*? He said that nearly two hours *before* they found the third murderee. And the third murderee was a brute-faced redhead!'

THE END

THE DETECTIVE STORY CLUB

FOR DETECTIVE CONNOISSEURS

recommends

"The Man with the Gun."

Philip MacDonald

Author of Rynox, etc.

MURDER GONE MAD

MR. MacDonald, who has shown himself in *The Noose* and *The Rasp* to be a master of the crime novel of pure detection, has here told a story of a motiveless crime, or at least a crime prompted only by blood lust. The sure, clear thinking of the individual detective is useless and only wide, cleverly organised investigation can hope to succeed.

A long knife with a brilliant but perverted brain directing it is terrorising Holmdale; innocent people are being done to death under the very eyes of the law. Inspector Pyke of Scotland Yard, whom MacDonald readers will remember in previous cases, is put on the track of the butcher. He has nothing to go on but the evidence of the bodies themselves and the butcher's own bravado. After every murder a businesslike letter arrives announcing that another "removal has been carried out." But Pyke "gets there" with a certainty the very slowness of which will give the reader many breathless moments. In the novelty of its treatment, the humour of its dialogue, and the truth of its characterisation, *Murder Gone Mad* is equal to the best Mr. MacDonald has written.

LOOK FOR THE MAN WITH THE GUN

THE DETECTIVE STORY CLUB

FOR DETECTIVE CONNOISSEURS

recommends

"The Man with the Gun."

The Murder of Roger Ackroyd
By AGATHA CHRISTIE

*T*HE MURDER OF ROGER ACKROYD is one of Mrs. Christie's most brilliant detective novels. As a play, under the title of *Alibi*, it enjoyed a long and successful run with Charles Laughton as the popular detective, Hercule Poirot. The novel has now been filmed, and its clever plot, skilful characterisation, and sparkling dialogue will make every one who sees the film want to read the book. M. Poirot, the hero of many brilliant pieces of detective deduction, comes out of his temporary retirement like a giant refreshed, to undertake the investigation of a peculiarly brutal and mysterious murder. Geniuses like Sherlock Holmes often find a use for faithful mediocrities like Dr. Watson, and by a coincidence it is the local doctor who follows Poirot round and himself tells the story. Furthermore, what seldom happens in these cases, he is instrumental in giving Poirot one of the most valuable clues to the mystery.

LOOK FOR THE MAN WITH THE GUN